'Where do you think you're going?'

'You know very well where; back to London.'

'And what about me?'

'Me! Mine!' Tasha spat the words at him. 'That's all you can say, isn't it? All you think about is yourself. *Your* disappointment, *your* frustration. Your lonely bed tonight. All you're interested in is satisfying your sexual cravings.'

Brett's jaw thrust forward. 'This is much more than just sex and you know it.'

'No, as a matter of fact, I don't know it. You're blinded by your own libido. You'll say anything to get what you want, because you're a typical male!'

Sally Wentworth was born and raised in Hertfordshire, where she still lives, and started writing after attending an evening class course. She is married and has one son. There is always a novel on the bedside table, but she also does craftwork, plays bridge, and is the president of a National Trust group. She goes to the ballet and theatre regularly and to open-air concerts in the summer. Sometimes she doesn't know how she finds the time to write!

Recent titles by the same author:

MARRIAGE BY ARRANGEMENT
CHRISTMAS NIGHTS
THE GUILTY WIFE

A TYPICAL MALE!

BY
SALLY WENTWORTH

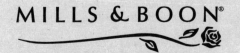

MILLS & BOON®

All the characters in this book have no existence outside the imagination of the author, and have no relation whatsoever to anyone bearing the same name or names. They are not even distantly inspired by any individual known or unknown to the author, and all the incidents are pure invention.

*First published in Great Britain 1997
Harlequin Mills & Boon Limited,
Eton House, 18-24 Paradise Road, Richmond, Surrey TW9 1SR*

© Sally Wentworth 1997

ISBN 0 263 80168 3

*Set in Times Roman 11 on 12 pt.
01-9707-50110 C1*

*Printed and bound in Great Britain
by Mackays of Chatham PLC, Chatham*

CHAPTER ONE

SHE looked wild! Sensational! Fascinating! As Brett King walked into the club where the party was being held his eyes were immediately drawn to the girl who danced under the spotlight. The band was playing 'Copacabana' to a rich tempo and the rest of the dancers on the floor had drawn back to watch as the girl in the red dress became one with the rhythm, her full skirt lifting as she swung, revealing legs that were long and very shapely. She bent and swayed with the beat, her long red hair a swirling flame that tantalisingly hid her face. Coloured strobe lights flickered across her slim body, adding to the impression of vibrant movement, of tropical heat and eroticism.

There were some steps that led down to the dance floor but Brett stayed where he was, his attention completely held. He noticed that the girl had a partner, who caught her and danced with her for a minute or so, but then she would step away from him and lose herself in the music again. And lose was the right word; she seemed totally unaware of the people who clapped and cheered her on, or of the effect her dance was having on those who watched.

It was certainly having an effect on Brett. He wondered if the girl knew how sexy, how extremely seductive she looked as she moved so sinuously in that bright heart of the dimly lit room. For a moment he

5

thought that she must be a professional dancer, but there was something unpolished and completely natural in the way she moved; it was all from the heart, the soul, not at all a technical, calculated performance. And it was when he realised this that Brett knew he had to meet her.

The music stopped at last and the girl was immediately surrounded by a crowd of laughing guests, congratulating her, wanting to touch her. Going down the steps, Brett first sought out the friend whose combined thirtieth birthday and leaving-London party this was.

'Hey, man, you're late,' Guy exclaimed when Brett finally found him and shook his hand.

'Got delayed,' Brett said vaguely.

'You look as if you need a drink.'

Brett laughed as he looked at his friend's already flushed face. 'You don't.'

'It's my birthday, for God's sake.'

They were almost shouting above the noise level of the crowded room and Brett had to lean closer as he said, 'Who was the girl?'

He didn't have to explain which girl. Guy grinned. 'She's really something, isn't she? Not many girls look that good when they let their hair down,' he remarked appreciatively.

'So who is she?'

'Her name's Natasha Briant. But you'll have to get in the queue; she's a popular girl.'

'Your girl?'

Guy laughed a little ruefully. 'No. You'll find she doesn't belong to anyone but herself—that's if you ever get close enough to find out, of course.'

Brett gave him a mock-derisive look. 'You questioning my style?'

'With your reputation for pulling women!' Guy threw up his hands in surrender. 'Would I dare?'

Laughing, Brett gave him a playful punch on the shoulder then went away to find himself a drink.

Leaning against the wall, drinking it, he saw that the girl, Natasha, also had a drink in her hand as she stood, still surrounded by a group of people, and he had to wait quite a while before she walked away from them to the ladies' cloakroom. Then he sauntered over and waited near the door until she came out.

'Hello, Natasha.'

She turned to look at him and he saw that her face went with the rest of her. Although not strictly beautiful, she had fine bone structure, a slightly pert nose, a mouth that fell into an easy smile and large, long-lashed eyes that were a very pale blue, almost aquamarine. Brilliant eyes, vital and alive.

Her glance went over him, frankly assessing, then she said in a husky-toned voice, 'We obviously haven't met before.'

His lips quirked. 'Why so sure?'

'No one I know ever calls me Natasha. It's always shortened to Tasha.'

The name was right for her, he thought, full of fire and passion. 'I bet you're descended from Russian gypsies.'

An amused look came into her eyes. 'Was I that gone?'

'Definitely. Is it your party piece?'

'Perhaps.' Her chin came up to challenge him. 'What's yours?'

His eyebrows rose at the opening she'd given him. A lesser man might have fallen for it and made some comment with sexual innuendo, but Brett recognised it for the test it was and smiled. 'I'm still working on one.'

'Have you so little talent?'

'Maybe I don't need to sing for my supper.'

'Are you implying that I do?' she challenged.

'I don't know. Why don't you come and have a drink so I can find out?'

Again Tasha looked at him in candid assessment. She quite liked what she saw; he was tall, over six feet, and in his early thirties, she guessed. His hair was thick and dark, a bit too long for him to be a yuppie like Guy, and he was good-looking in a casual, laid-back kind of way. She was about to refuse when it occurred to her that the casualness was deceptive, his lean figure spoke of coiled-steel strength and there was determination in the set of his chin. To test him, she shook her head. 'No, thanks. I'm with some people.'

'So leave them.'

'Why should I?'

'How do you know you won't always regret it if you don't?'

She laughed at that. 'That sounds like a well-rehearsed line.'

'Are you married? Engaged? Living with someone?'

At each question Tasha gave a slow shake of her

head, her eyes quizzical. 'Do you already feel such rapport between us, then?' she asked in amusement.

'No. But if you don't have anyone, then you can't find the people you're with very interesting. So what have you got to lose by having a drink with me?'

'Am I likely to find you interesting?'

'Yes.'

Her eyebrows rose but Tasha rather liked the blunt answer. 'Such modesty,' she mocked.

'I find that false modesty never gets you very far.' He held out his right hand. 'I'm Brett King. Guy and I were at university together. I'm unattached, straight, and more or less respectable.' He could have added that he was not only intrigued by but greatly attracted to her, but he didn't, guessing rightly that such a remark would immediately put her off.

She shook his hand, found his grip firm but relaxed. 'And are you a whiz-kid in the world of finance?'

'Definitely not.'

'Good heavens! Why didn't you say so before? In that case I'll certainly have a drink.'

'Good.' He smiled, the grin making his face more boyish, less lived-in. 'Shall we go somewhere quieter?'

Tasha pointed to the mezzanine floor where small tables overlooked the dancing area. 'We'll go up there.'

Brett had wanted to leave the party altogether, take her some place else where they could talk in peace, but he willingly settled for the mezzanine. He took a bottle of champagne and a couple of glasses from the bar and they found a free table against the wall.

'So what have you got against whiz-kids from the City?'

'They fancy themselves too much.'

'Guy's one of them.'

'Yes, but he's nice. We'll all miss him now he's going to be based in Hong Kong.'

'How do you know him?' he asked.

Tasha shrugged. 'He's one of the crowd. He used to go out with a girl I worked with and he became a friend.'

'What do you do?'

'I thought this conversation was supposed to be about you—about how interesting you are,' she reminded him.

'Don't tell me you don't like talking about yourself?'

'I already know all about me.'

That made him laugh. 'Unnatural woman!'

'So what do you do?'

Brett could have given her a very long list of the things he'd done with his life, but settled for the latest. 'I'm a writer.'

Tasha's interest immediately sharpened. 'Successful?' she asked suspiciously.

Brett grimaced. 'I suppose it depends on what you mean by successful. I've had two novels published and I've just finished a third. They weren't overnight bestsellers by any means, but they sold in quite respectable numbers.'

'Enough to encourage you to go on, obviously.'

He nodded. 'But not enough to lash out on a luxury

pad in Chelsea or drive a Porsche like Guy,' he re-marked, setting a test of his own.

With a dismissive gesture of her hand Tasha rubbed out Guy's and his colleagues' efforts. 'Those people burn themselves out by the time they're forty, if not earlier. Tell me about your books. Are they thrillers?'

He frowned. 'Not really. All three have been different. The first one had quite a bit of action in it, but the second was a sort of search into a person's mind to find out why he did what he did, what made him the kind of person who would commit a terrible crime.' He shrugged. 'You probably know the kind of thing. It's certainly nothing new.'

'And the latest?'

'I'm not going to tell you about that one.'

'Why not?'

'If I tell you everything in one go you won't find me interesting any more.'

She smiled, but said on a note of satisfaction, 'At least I've found out that you're a serious writer. Did you base the books on your own experience?'

Brett saw from the way she leaned forward, her eyes on his face, that she really wanted to know, she wasn't just being polite. Gratified, pleased that he'd got her attention so easily, he said, 'Not directly. The first one was based on a true story, something that happened to a friend of mine, but the second and third were pure fiction.' He enlarged a little but something held him back from telling her that he had used his experiences as a journalist to feed his imagination. Perhaps because she was obviously awed by his being a serious writer and he didn't want to detract from that. There would be plenty of time to tell her his life story, if he could hold her interest enough now to get her to agree to see him again. And he found that he wanted that very much.

'How did you go about finding a publisher?' Tasha asked him.

'With great difficulty.' He spread his hands. Strong, capable hands, she noticed. 'I had a few contacts— friends who knew someone in the trade, that kind of thing. I tried those first, without any success. But then I was lucky enough to find an agency that was interested in the story and they eventually sold it for me.'

'You *were* lucky. I've heard that it's a sort of Catch 22 situation with agents; they'll only take you on if you've had something accepted, but how do you get accepted if you haven't got an agent?'

'You almost sound as if you speak from your own experience.'

She gave a small shrug but didn't deny it.

'So what do you do?'

'I work in the research department of a television company. Not the BBC, before you ask. A smaller, independent company.' She watched as he refilled her glass. 'I really don't think I ought to have much more of that.' She gave a mischievous grin. 'But it *is* good champagne.'

Brett smiled back. 'And we owe it to Guy to give him a good send-off.'

'Absolutely.'

He loved the way she said the word, stressing the vowels in that gorgeously husky voice. He found he couldn't decide what about her attracted him most:

her vitality, those sensational legs, her face and extraordinary eyes, or that seductive voice. Maybe it was everything, that all the elements combined to make an irresistible whole.

It was a heady thought and one that left him feeling not only excited but rather overwhelmed. He wasn't used to being bowled over just by looking at a woman. Maybe he'd been around too long, had affairs with too many women and become blasé. Trying to dispel the feeling, Brett resorted to the commonplace as he said, 'So what are you researching at the moment?'

To his surprise imps of mischief danced in her eyes and she leaned forward to whisper, 'I can't tell you. It's top secret!' She said the last two words in an American drawl, glancing at him from under her lashes to see how he would react.

Delighted, Brett pretended extreme seriousness as he said, 'Beheading at dawn in the Tower stuff, huh?'

'And some. Heads will definitely roll.'

'Sounds to me like you need a bodyguard.'

She gave him a pert look. 'Who would you suggest?'

He grinned, rubbed the side of his jaw. 'I think I've entrapped myself here. Something tells me you wouldn't like it if I suggested myself. But then—' he paused deliberately '—I wouldn't like it if you chose someone else.'

He kept his eyes on her as he spoke, watching to see how she would take it, but Tasha only laughed and finished the wine in her glass. 'I want to dance.'

She rose and headed for the stairs, to his chagrin not looking to see whether he followed her or not.

But he caught her up on the edge of the dance floor and took a firm hold of her hand as he pulled her into his arms. Tasha stiffened, and for a moment he thought she was going to resist, but then she relaxed and let him lead her. It was a slow number and the floor was crowded; there was room only to smooch around, held close against each other. Several people spoke to Tasha, both men and women, and all seemed pleased to see her, but no one greeted Brett.

'You don't seem to know many people here,' she commented.

'I don't. Guy's the only one. We don't really see each other much now—just occasionally for a drink or something.'

'Is it a very solitary life—being a writer?'

He shrugged. 'When you're working it has to be, but the rest of the time you can be as sociable as anyone else.'

'Do you live alone?'

'Yes.' He wondered if that was a loaded question, whether it meant she fancied him.

But evidently it wasn't, because Tasha gave a small frown and said, 'When you live alone you need friends, but friends take a lot of work, a lot of time.'

'That sounds very philosophical.' He glanced down at her, but he didn't have to lower his head too much, she came up to his chin. Just the right height for kissing. The soft aroma of her perfume, like the tantalising scent of an orchid, filled his senses and Brett wanted badly to kiss her.

'Not really. It's just that—' she gave a small shrug '—sometimes you need time for yourself, to be alone to do what you want to do—like write. Don't you find that?'

Tasha glanced up and found Brett gazing at her intently. There was a look in his eyes that she recognised, a look she had seen in many men's eyes before: hungry, concupiscent. Their eyes met and she raised a mocking, slightly derisive eyebrow. Brett laughed, in no way embarrassed at being caught out, and not at all ashamed of the way he was feeling. But he said, 'Yes. Writers can be pretty insular people. Even when I'm not writing I spend a lot of time walking around, thinking out plots, characters, that kind of thing.'

'Do you have lots of friends who interrupt you all the time?'

'I can shut them out. Just turn on the answering machine and ignore the doorbell.'

'That's the quickest way I know to lose your friends.'

'You have to live your life the way you want to live it, not for other people.'

Tasha gave an ironical laugh. 'Now who's being philosophical?'

'Yeah.' His mouth twisted a little as he smiled down at her.

He had, she noticed, a very attractive smile, and his brown eyes were warm and caressing. The band began to play 'Lady in Red' and Brett's arm slid further round her waist as he drew her closer. 'This should be your tune,' he murmured, touching the strap of her red dress, his fingers briefly stroking the bare skin of her shoulder.

Tasha smiled inwardly but didn't resist. He was right in thinking that she'd find him interesting, and he seemed different from most of the men who seemed to come her way. There was an inner strength in him which she could sense but which he deliberately seemed to want to hide behind his casual manner. That alone would have aroused her curiosity, but the fact that he was a published writer had also intrigued her. And he fancied her, of course, but she'd realised that from the first moment he'd spoken to her.

That she was attractive to men, Tasha knew; she had come to look on it as just one of those things you were born with, like having red hair and being five feet eight inches tall. But she had learned how to handle it, how to use it to her advantage when she wanted to, and how to squash flat men she found boring. It had also got her into a few tight corners when she was younger, experiences she'd prefer to forget, but she had learned from them and now, at twenty-four, was pretty confident of her ability to take care of herself.

The music changed to a hotter beat and they danced apart. She was pleased to find that Brett moved well, that he danced as loosely as the surface impression he gave, but the alertness was still there, as he proved when he caught her hand to pull her quickly out of the way of a couple who'd drunk too much and were all wildly gyrating arms and kicking legs. Keeping hold of her hand, he shouted in her ear, 'Why don't we get out of this?'

Tasha hesitated only briefly before nodding. 'OK. But I want to say goodbye to Guy first.'

They found him propped up against the bar, literally propped up by a couple of friends as he looked in danger of sliding to the floor. He gave them a huge grin as they came up. 'Tasha, my darling!' He pulled one arm free and put it round her.

'Thanks, Guy, it's been a great party.'

'You're not going? You can't go! It's still early.'

'I'm afraid so. Every success in Hong Kong, Guy. Don't lose too many billions on the futures market, will you?'

'No, I can't let you go.' A look of great tragedy came into his face. 'I'm going to tell them I'm not going. I can't leave all my friends like this.'

'Nonsense,' Tasha soothed. 'You'll love it there. And we'll all come out and visit you. Or else you can phone.'

She managed to get away, but not until Guy had kissed her with maudlin sentimentality. Brett shook his hand and wished him well and then they made for the door. But when they reached it they met up with half a dozen other people who were also leaving, friends of Tasha's, who insisted they go along with them for something to eat. Brett would have refused but Tasha cast a laughing glance at him and agreed at once. Piling into a couple of taxis, they drove to a backstreet café, a place of metal tables, wooden floor and condensation running down the windows. 'Have the all-day breakfast,' Tasha urged him.

'It's three o'clock in the morning,' Brett pointed out.

'So what better time to have it? You'll be ahead of yourself. Go on, the food here is fantastic.'

They ordered and pushed a couple of tables together, drank beer with their bacon and eggs and sausages, which were, Brett had to admit, excellent. There were other customers in the café: taxi drivers having a break, workers from the nearby mainline station and a couple of nurses from the private hospital down the street. One of the latter asked Tasha for the salt cellar and she passed it over with a sympathetic smile, saying, 'You poor things, you look worn out. Have you just finished work?'

'Yes. Ten hours we've been on.'

'Really? Surely you shouldn't have to work that long?'

'We do if we want to keep our jobs.'

Tasha started chatting to them, then moved over to sit at their table, Brett and the others forgotten.

'She's always doing that,' one of her friends explained to Brett.

He nodded, unworried. Soon they would leave and then he would get her alone. He watched her with a slightly amused look in his eyes. She was a good listener and the nurses were really opening up to her as she smiled and nodded in sympathy, asked a question or gave a horrified gasp at an answer. Watching the play of emotions in her face, he became fascinated all over again. He was reminded of an old song, something about falling in love across a crowded room. He didn't know if what he'd felt when he first saw Tasha was love but she had certainly had a devastating effect on his senses. But maybe she made that impression on all men. A 'honey-pot' effect, he thought. Something that drew men to her. He'd met a couple of other women like that in the past and had been attracted, but only briefly because there was no substance beneath the sexiness. But he rather thought that Tasha was different.

The others rose to leave and he stood up, holding out his hand to Tasha. She glanced up. He stood very tall beside her, but there was nothing looming about it, and the extended hand was an invitation not a command. With a small smile she put her own in it, said goodbye to the nurses, and went outside with him.

Dawn was breaking. The misty pink glow of the rising sun brushed the deserted streets and sleeping houses, softening any harshness, giving warmth and light to the darkness. They all gathered on the pavement for a few minutes to say goodbye, then peeled off in couples to search for cabs to take them home this early on a Sunday morning.

'Where to?' Brett asked her.

Tasha looked round, then said, 'I don't really want to go home. I'd like to walk by the river.'

'Aren't you tired?'

'No. Oh, dear! Does that mean you are?'

'No.' And it was true; tonight he was on such a high that it was impossible to feel tired.

She slid her arm through his in a completely natural gesture. 'Good. Where do you live?'

'I've got a place in Docklands.'

'And is that where you write?'

'Most of the time. But I've also got an old cottage

by the coast in Cornwall; sometimes I go down there and shut myself away.'

'Oh, I envy you that!' Tasha exclaimed. 'How marvellous it must be to get up when you feel like it, work without any interruptions and... Do you have a phone there?'

'A mobile,' Brett admitted. 'But I switch it off most of the time.'

'So you can shut the world out,' she said with satisfaction. 'How about a computer?'

'A lap-top'.

'So you do take twentieth-century technology with you?'

'Did you imagine I'd be bashing out the stories with two fingers on an old typewriter?'

Tasha shook her head. 'Not really. I suppose we're children of the computer age. I'm often stuck in front of one for days at a time. But it would be wonderful to be able to shut yourself away.'

'Don't you like people?'

'Oh, yes, of course.' She paused, looked as if she was about to say something, but then shook her head.

Brett, feeling that this was important, that what she might have said would have given a clue to her character and very much wanting to know her better, said persuasively, 'Tell me.'

Again she shook her head. 'No, I don't know you well enough.' And she moved to take her arm from his.

They had come to the river and were walking along the Embankment. They were completely alone. Brett came to a halt in a shaft of sunlight and turned her to face him. The sun caught her hair, turning it into a stream of molten gold. She looked so lovely his breath caught for a moment in his throat. But then he pulled himself together and said firmly, 'That's very strange—because I feel as if I've always known you. All my life.' Reaching out, he took her hand. 'You can trust me, Tasha. I think you know that.'

'Do I?' She looked up into his face for a long moment. Then gave a small, awkward laugh. 'Please don't get serious.' There was a note of pleading in her voice.

Immediately sensing it, Brett grinned, lightening the moment. 'I'm not. But you're hiding from me.'

Nearby there was one of the ornate wrought-iron bench seats that were placed at intervals along the Embankment. Tasha drew her hand out of his and went to sit on it. She leaned forward pensively, her elbow on her knee and her chin balanced on her fist. Brett leaned back against the parapet, watching her, waiting.

There was mist still hovering over the river but it was clearing rapidly as the sun rose, grew warmer. A solitary working boat chugged downstream towards the estuary and the sea, with a black cat that sat on the stern, washing its fur, completely at home on the water. It made Tasha smile and she suddenly felt good. The cat, the morning sun, and Brett—yes, she had to admit he made her feel pretty good, too. He certainly looked good, leaning back like that, his hands in his trouser pockets, the material stretched tight across his hips. Her throat felt dry for a moment and she quickly lifted her eyes to his face. And she liked the firm set of his jaw, its square determination, his lazy-lidded eyes. But could she trust him as he'd said?

Tasha was a creature of instinct, although instinct had proved to be wrong in the past and she'd learned not to trust it. But, impulsively, she did so now, saying slowly, 'Do you ever feel that life is like a long corridor—a corridor of closed doors?'

'Is that how you feel?'

She nodded. 'Sometimes the doors are opened for you; sometimes you open them yourself.'

'And when you go through them?' Brett asked, his eyes fixed intently on her face.

She gave a small shrug. 'Sometimes it's bright and sunlit and you're glad you opened the door. But sometimes it's dark and cold.' She was silent for a moment, lost in thought, lost in past memories, then she looked up at him. 'After you've opened those kinds of doors it makes you more careful. Instead of opening every door you choose to walk past some of them, leave them closed.'

He came to sit beside her, put his hand on the back of the seat as he faced her. Softly he said, 'But how do you know which ones to open and which to leave closed?'

'You don't; that's just the trouble.' For a moment her beautiful eyes became very vulnerable. 'That's why you're always afraid.'

'Of what?'

'Of not opening the door that might lead you to—' She stopped abruptly.

Instead of pushing her to tell him, he said gently,

'To the ultimate door?' She didn't answer so he guessed. 'The one that leads to happiness for the rest of your life?'

Entranced that he had read her mind, Tasha gave him the most wonderful smile. 'Yes, the one that leads to paradise,' she said simply.

He was astonished that she'd chosen that word, that she still believed that there could be such a place. He saw that she was, at heart, still an innocent, still a believer in perfect happiness, even though she'd hinted at a knowledge of the darker side of life. This new perception of her—and that smile—caught at his heart.

She saw the astonishment in his face and looked away. As if she regretted having confided in him, Tasha suddenly got to her feet and began to walk along at a brisk pace. Thinking that she was upset, Brett quickly caught her up. But she smiled at him and said, 'I just looked at Big Ben and saw the time. It's nearly six. I must find a cab.'

He wondered if that was just an excuse; she'd seemed in no hurry before. But he said, 'We'll get one in Trafalgar Square.'

Five minutes later they picked one up, the driver on his way home after working all night. 'Where do you live?' Brett asked her.

'In Bloomsbury. Within spitting distance of the British Museum.'

'Handy for research.'

Tasha got in the cab and Brett went to follow her, but she said, 'Look, you really don't have to—'

But he said, 'Don't be silly,' and got in beside her.

In the taxi they talked about Guy, Brett telling her some amusing anecdotes about him from the time they were at university together. He spoke entertainingly but without doing Guy down, which she liked; she got annoyed if people were cruel just to get a laugh at a story. But Brett spoke quite naturally, there was nothing forced or over the top. He didn't put on an act, and he seemed to get as much enjoyment out of remembering the incidents as she did from hearing them. He was obviously fond of Guy and didn't mind her seeing it, and she liked that too.

Tasha began to wonder about him, about his background, if he was very experienced with women. Somehow she thought he would be, he was so self-confident, so assured in his manner towards her. She knew he was attracted to her, he'd made that very obvious, but he wasn't pushing it too much. There had been that one incident when he'd told her he felt he'd known her a long time; that disturbed her—was playing it too fast. Because she wasn't yet at all sure that this was a door she wanted to open.

Her eyes were fixed reflectively on his face and she saw his eyebrow rise in amusement and realised he had stopped speaking. 'Was it such a boring story?' he said ruefully.

Tasha laughed. 'Sorry, I was thinking.'

'Dare I ask what about?'

Smiling, she shook her head.

'Was it about me?'

The smile became mocking. 'Why would I be thinking about you when there are a million other things I could be thinking of?'

He pretended to groan and put his hand over his heart. 'That put me in my place. And there was I, hoping that I'd made an indelible impression on you.'

Tasha couldn't resist asking, 'Are you used to making an impression on women?'

Reaching over, Brett took hold of her hand and began to play with her fingers. 'That, if I may so, Miss Briant, is a very loaded question. Whatever I say I can't win. I'll either look a wimp or an egotist.'

'So?'

'So—I'm not going to answer it.'

She laughed. 'Wasn't it you, I seem to remember, who said you didn't believe in false modesty? So that must mean that you're a wi—' She broke off as Brett put a finger over her lips.

His brown eyes laughed down at her. 'I can see I'm going to have trouble with you.'

She put her hand over his and drew it away a little, said playfully, 'Who, sir? Me, sir?'

'Yes, you.' He stroked the back of his fingers down her cheek as his gaze held hers, became intent. He leaned forward as if to kiss her, but just then the taxi drew up and the driver, eager to get home, shouted, 'We're here.'

Tasha laughed up at him, enjoying the chagrin in his face. But when he reached for the door handle and looked as if he was going to get out, she became instantly serious again and stopped him, saying, 'You may as well keep the cab to take you home.'

He looked at her for a moment, taking in the implications, but his face didn't change as he shook his head. 'I'll see you to your door.'

They got out of the taxi and Brett paid it off, then turned towards her, not quite knowing what to expect. Even that feeling was almost a stranger to him; he wasn't used to being unsure of himself, and definitely not to being rejected. When the cab drove away they stood and looked at each other, Brett being careful not to be the first to speak. Then he saw her begin to smile and he was filled with hope.

'Do you have a heart condition?'

Startled, he said, 'Good heavens, no!'

'You don't suffer from asthma or anything like that?'

'Just how old do you think I am?' he said indignantly.

'OK. But don't say you haven't been warned.'

They were standing outside an imposing terrace of six-storey Victorian houses, with large bay windows and solid front doors with ornate fanlights over them, in a prosperous-looking street. But, instead of using the front door, Tasha went down some steps to the basement area where she unlocked a door that gave onto a long corridor, evidently what had once been the servants' entrance to the house. She led him down the corridor to a narrow back stair and gave him an impish grin as she began to run up them.

She lived on the very top floor, in the attics, and even Brett, who considered himself to be pretty fit and had taken the stairs two at a time, was feeling winded when they reached it. But Tasha wasn't even out of breath.

'How long have you lived here?' he demanded as

he leaned against the wall while she unlocked her door.

She grinned. 'Two years. An Olympic athlete would envy the muscles in my legs,' she told him.

'No wonder you dance so well.'

The door opened straight into a huge sitting-room that ran the width of the house. The windows were uncurtained, letting the morning sunlight flood the room, so that Brett's first impression was of light and warmth. He became aware of bright colours, of a red shawl draped across a settee, of a Mexican rug in greens and blues on the bleached and polished wood of the floor. There were a great many pictures on three of the white-painted walls, modern pictures of clear-cut shapes and colours. The fourth wall was hidden behind primitive but practical bookshelves made of wooden planks supported by tiers of red bricks. There were a great many books, some with the lurid-coloured jackets of novels, others with the more staid covers of reference books.

There wasn't much furniture, he noticed, just the settee, a table in front of the window with a couple of old dining-chairs, and another series of bricks and planks across one corner to hold a television set and a music system. It was a clean, uncluttered place, but full of warmth and colour. Like the character of its owner? Brett wondered, and was more intrigued than ever.

Tasha began to say, 'If you'd like a coffee or some-thing—' but Brett caught her arm as she went to move away and pulled her towards him.

'What's the ''or something''?'

'Tea?' she suggested.

He smiled, put his arms round her and held her eyes as he drew her close. Unexpectedly, he found that his heart was beating too fast and he was full of the intoxicating excitement of anticipation—emotions he hadn't experienced for a very long time. His lips were dry and his hands unsteady; he felt like a teenager on his first date and just as nervous. Her eyes were open and there was an almost wary look in their blue depths. Softly, reassuringly, he said her name, 'Tasha,' on a long, unsteady breath. Then he reached up to gently touch her face before he bent his head and found her lips.

She had been kissed many times before by many men, both passionately and gently, and didn't expect this to be much different. Perhaps he might be a little more experienced, but Tasha went into that kiss with her eyes wide open in every meaning of the phrase. His hand went round the back of her head to hold her closer and slowly her eyes closed as his lips moved against hers. It was almost as if she could feel his heart in his lips, slightly trembling, searching, wanting to reach her soul and awaken it from the safety of slumber. His lips were warm, vital, infinitely caressing. They weren't gentle and not yet passionate, but teasing and evocative.

A sudden longing filled her, a yearning that she had dreamed about but never known. She relaxed a little and felt a tremor run through him, whether of triumph or libido, she didn't know. Because her own body was starting to awaken, to let desire take hold. Her lips moved under his and she began to kiss him in return.

Brett breathed her name again on a soft groan, and moved his lips to her throat, trailing kisses along its length, but then came back to her lips again, avid for the response he wanted. Her hand went to his neck and she could feel his pulse beating there, wild and erratic. He rained tantalising little kisses on her lips and she opened her mouth, letting him into its secret warmth. Tasha felt her senses begin to whirl, stood on the edge of the vortex knowing that if she let herself drown in the growing demands of her own body, in her need of him, then she would be taking an irreversible step, would be opening a door through which she couldn't see. With a low moan, she stepped back from the edge, drew away and held him at arm's length.

'I think you'd better stop,' she said, on an unsteady but firm note.

Disappointment engulfed him and he was sharply tempted to just ignore her and pull her back into his arms. To *force* her to want him as much as he wanted her. To overcome her resistance with more kisses until she changed her mind, until she cried out for him to take her. But one look at her face drove all chauvinism from his mind. There was a shocked look in her face, as if she had been taken entirely by surprise. But that the surprise had been pleasant he could see by the warmth in her startled eyes. So maybe there was hope yet, if he didn't rush things, if he played it cool. But he still said, 'Are you sure?' on a hopeful note.

Tasha laughed at him. 'Yes, I'm quite sure.' She moved away from him. 'I'm going to change.' She went to a door in the wall away from the window. 'If you want a coffee before you go, the kitchen's through here.'

'Are you going to bed?'

'Good heavens, no.' She gave him a surprised look. 'I'm going to get ready for work.'

'Work! On a Sunday morning?'

'That's when the people I have to interview for my television programme are usually at home.'

She left him and Brett wandered after her. He was in an inner corridor, the first door leading into the kitchen. It was very small and compact, made out of what once must have been a large linen cupboard, he guessed. He switched on the kettle and, curious, went on down the corridor. Behind one door he could hear the sound of a shower running and guessed that was the bathroom. There were two other doors. One opened into a bedroom at the back of the house. Here one wall was entirely taken up by built-in wardrobes painted in a soft green. There was a bed that could have been either a large single or a small double and which, the way he was feeling at the moment, looked an infinitely good place to be—so long as Tasha was there with him. There was also a dressing table, more bookshelves, and a large ottoman at the foot of the bed. Again the place was very clean and tidy and the colours, although not making as bold a statement as in the sitting-room, were warm and inviting.

When he opened the door of the last room, also at the back of the house, Brett smiled. He'd read somewhere that you had to see where a person worked to really know them, and this was evidently where Tasha worked. There was a huge desk under the window and it was piled with papers, folders and a great many books, jostling for space with a computer and all the bits that went with it, a fax and a telephone. There were filing cabinets with the drawers open and a great many more books and papers on the floor, as if tossed there because she was too impatient to get on with what she was working on to put them away. On one wall there were a couple of cork noticeboards, both covered in pieces of papers, lists, letters and reminders. It was the work-room of a very busy person, and he began to understand now why she'd said she envied him the cottage in Cornwall.

Idly Brett picked up a couple of the folders from the desk and glanced at their titles. One was, he saw with interest, an idea for a programme on the follow-up of young men who'd had testicular cancer, how they had coped and how it had affected their lives. He could imagine that making a very popular programme. Another was on Car Boot sales and their growing popularity. 'Will they eventually kill off the church jumble sale?' Tasha had written on it.

Brett gave a small smile and put down the folder. There was another one on the desk, partly open. He caught the words 'Sexual Exploitation' at the top of a sheet of paper and, his interest caught, he pulled it out. There was a long list of names, all women, under the words, 'To be interviewed'. The names meant nothing but the few scribbled words alongside each of them suddenly meant a great deal. 'Sec. to MD, Sampson Holdings', he read. And, 'Researcher to Lord Moggach, HOL', followed by, 'PA to Principal, Univ. of Westshire'. Brett's eyes widened incredu-

lously as he read down the list. My God, this was
dynamite! Here were listed the names of some of the
most important men in the business establishment—
and in politics, he realised as he recognised that HOL
meant House of Lords and, further down the page,
HOC was House of Commons.

He gave an astounded whistle under his breath. His
journalist's mind immediately foresaw what could
happen. If Tasha interviewed all these women and got
stories of sexual exploitation from them—from even
a quarter of them!—it would be a scandal that would
rock the country. But surely all these women would
never reveal their secrets to a television reporter, even
if they had a secret to tell. But Tasha wasn't just any
television reporter; Brett remembered her talking to
the nurses in the café, how they had responded to her
warmth and sympathy, telling her, a complete
stranger, the details of their working lives, and of their
own lives, too, he recalled. He stood, staring into his
own mind, as he realised that she was the ideal person
for a job like this; the genuine warmth in her character, that air of innocence in her eyes—who would
hesitate to take her into their confidence, to help her
and tell her all she wanted to know? Especially
woman to woman. And many women might be more
than happy to have a means of revenge in the endless
war of the sexes.

The sound of the shower stopped and he hastily put
down the folder in exactly the same place and went
softly back to the kitchen, remembering to shut the
door of the work-room quietly behind him. The kettle
had boiled and he made himself a coffee, took it back

into the sitting-room. He had just finished drinking it when Tasha came back in. She had changed into a neat, dark business suit with a skirt well below her knees but with a slit up the side that revealed sheer black tights above her high-heeled shoes. Her hair was drawn back into a plait and she had remade up her face with subtler shades of lipstick and eyeshadow. So this was Tasha Briant, career-woman; she looked a completely different girl from the one who had danced with such natural passion just a few hours ago.

She looked a little surprised to find him still there, but smiled and said, 'I'm ready to roll.'

He got to his feet. 'I'll lean on you while we go down all those stairs.'

Tasha laughed. 'Once up and down those is usually enough to convince my dates that they never want to see me again.'

Brett realised she was giving him an opening, a laughing way of saying that he agreed and that it had been nice but it was over. But he thought of the folder he'd seen and knew that he was not only going to see her again, he was going to get close—as close as a lover.

CHAPTER TWO

WHEN they reached the street Brett paused and said, 'Where are you heading?'

'I've an appointment to see someone near Bath.'

In his mind he rapidly ran through the list of names he'd seen and figured out she was probably going to see the secretary of the university head. 'By train?'

'No, by car.'

There were cars parked on both sides of the road with 'Resident Parking' stickers on their windscreens and he glanced at them, wondering which one was hers. 'What do you drive?'

'I've got a little Fiat coupé.'

'A sports car? Aren't you afraid of having it stolen?'

Tasha laughed. 'No. I'll show you. This way.'

She led him to the end of the terrace and down what must have once been a carriageway that led to the back of the houses. A security gate barred the way but Tasha unlocked a door at the side of it and Brett saw that there were rows of stables that had been converted into garages. Tasha's garage was almost at the end of the row and the Fiat was a bright buttercup-yellow. He laughed. 'And there was I, guessing your car would just have to be red.'

'So as not to clash with my hair, you mean?' She gave a groan and put her hand up to her head. 'It's the bane of my life.'

'Don't be ridiculous! Your hair is glorious.'

She smiled her appreciation of the compliment but only said, 'Can I give you a lift?'

Brett could easily have walked to the nearest tube station but he wasn't going to pass up a chance to be with her for a little longer—or to ride in that car.

He was almost too tall for the car, but he had only been sitting in it a few minutes, while he listened to the acceleration and the engine, before he knew that he liked it. 'It's quite a car,' he acknowledged. 'Are you sure you're awake enough to drive all the way to Bath?'

Tasha's lips twisted in amusement. 'Oh, sure, I'm fine.'

'I'm not doing anything special today; I could come with you and give you a break, if you like?'

She laughed openly. 'Admit it; you've fallen in love with the car!'

That was an opening for a flattering compliment if not something far deeper if ever he'd heard one, but Brett didn't fall into the trap. Instead he grinned in return and said, 'You should feel very sorry for me; I only have a beaten up four-wheel drive model. I have to park on the street and anything else would get either stolen or vandalised.'

'Ah, I feel so sorry for you,' she mocked.

'So you should.' His voice had softened because he'd turned to look at her and seen that a wayward tendril of hair had escaped and now caressed the line of her cheek. He would have liked to reach out and touch it but knew better than to do so. 'So, do I come with you?'

'No.' She shook her head but there was no real

rejection in her tone. She pulled into the kerb and Brett saw they were outside a tube station. 'I'm meeting someone for lunch.'

'So when will I see you again?' Behind them a red double-decker, unable to get by, honked impatiently. One didn't argue with a London bus. Brett got out quickly but ducked down to look in the door. 'When?' he demanded.

But Tasha only lifted a hand in hurried farewell. 'If I don't get out of the way he'll ram me. Bye.'

He had no choice but to let her go, and stood on the pavement, inwardly fuming, as he watched her pull away.

It was almost a week before Brett saw Tasha again. She had proved to be singularly elusive. Figuring that she wouldn't be back from Bath until late, he hadn't tried to phone her until the evening and then, to his annoyance, had found that her number was ex-directory. His only contact with her was Guy, so the next day Brett had gone to his flat, but the place was empty, the caretaker telling him that Guy had already moved out and gone to stay with his parents for a few days until his departure for Hong Kong. And Tasha hadn't told him the name of the company she worked for, so that was no help. In the end he had managed to trace Guy's parents' address and had rung him there.

'Tasha's phone number?' Guy laughed. 'Wouldn't she give it to you? Maybe I shouldn't let you have it, then.'

'Cut it, Guy. Just tell me the number.'

'This could cost you; I shall need somewhere to stay when I come over to London and—'

'You can stay,' Brett interrupted. 'Stay as long as you like. Now give me the number.'

Again laughing with enjoyment, Guy said, 'You *have* got it badly. All right, I'll get it for you.' He paused a moment and his voice had changed to a warning as he added, 'But be careful, Brett.'

'What do you mean?'

'Just that... Well, other men have fallen for Tasha, fallen heavily, but I haven't yet known her let anyone get really close.'

It was impossible not to wonder if Guy was referring to himself, but Brett didn't ask. He wrote down the number Guy gave him and immediately rang it. All he got was a message on the answering machine. It was admittedly in Tasha's gorgeously husky voice but the tone was businesslike. He became used to that tone over the next three days, because it was always the recording that answered. And Tasha didn't return his calls. The first two or three times he left messages giving her his number and asking her to call him back, but after that he just replaced the receiver without speaking.

At first he thought that she was probably out doing an interview or at work; he made excuses for her, but after a couple of days he began to feel first angry, then anxious. Was this her way of letting him know that she didn't want to see him again? But he *had* to see her again. Brett cursed himself for behaving like a lovesick schoolboy, but found that he couldn't concentrate on his work and kept looking moodily at the phone, trying by sheer will-power to make it ring. He could imagine himself stretching out his hand to lift the receiver, saying hello and hearing her voice, so husky and intimate, telling him that she was sorry, that she'd been away, had only just got back. But the phone didn't ring.

In the end, unable to stand it any longer, he threw pride out of the window and went round to her flat. It took him a while to find it because when they'd gone there before she hadn't given the taxi-driver her exact address, had just told him to go to the British Museum and had directed him from there. And when they'd driven away together there had been a van obscuring the sign showing the name of the road. So he had to drive around the streets until he eventually found it, but when he rang the bell beside her name there was no answer and his spirits fell to zero again. He decided to wait.

It was almost three hours later and day had turned into evening before he saw the little yellow sports car turn into the driveway between the houses, and another few minutes before Tasha appeared and walked along the pavement. Not that most people would have known it was her, because her top half was completely obscured behind the large framed picture she was carrying. But Brett had no difficulty—he recognised her legs.

He had intended to wait until she got to her flat but instead got out of his car and crossed the street to meet her. She couldn't see him so he peered at her over the top of the frame. 'I heard the *Mona Lisa* had been stolen,' he remarked.

'Brett!' Tasha looked surprised to see him, but not at all embarrassed, he noted. 'Oh, good. I was just thinking that I could do with some muscle to carry this.'

She handed over the picture, which he saw was a modern, cubist still-life. 'Haven't you got enough pictures on your walls—or are you planning on opening a gallery?'

'I saw it in a second-hand shop and couldn't resist it.'

'Is it the real thing?'

'No, only a signed print, unfortunately. Do you like it?'

Brett held it out in front of him, his head tilted to one side in consideration, as they went down the steps to the door of her building. 'Yes. Yes, I do. And are you going to give me the great pleasure of carrying it up all those stairs to your place?'

Tasha laughed. 'Of course.' She gave him a mischievous look. 'But you will be suitably rewarded.'

'I suppose that means you'll give me the kiss of life if I pass out at the top,' he said wryly, which made her laugh again.

But when they reached her flat she immediately made him hold the picture in several different places until she decided just where she wanted it hung. 'Are you any good at knocking in picture hooks?' she asked hopefully.

He held out a hand. 'Where's the hammer?' he asked resignedly.

When the picture was in place they both stood back to admire it. Brett longed to ask her why she hadn't returned his calls, and he also badly wanted to know just how far she'd got with her research into the sexual exploitation programme, but instead he said,

'Do you deliberately leave yourself open to suggestive remarks?'

Tasha gave him an amused look, her mouth twisting into the exact smile of the *Mona Lisa* he'd accused her of stealing. 'You don't rise to the bait,' she admitted.

'What would happen if I did?'

'Nothing.'

'Just—nothing?' She nodded, watching him, and he couldn't resist saying, 'Not a lot seems to be happening now.'

Then she completely startled and delighted him by saying, 'But you're here,' and coming to put her arms round his neck and kissing him, her lips soft and sensuous under his. But after all too short a moment she stepped back, her eyes teasing. 'And that was your reward.'

'Was it?' Reaching out, Brett caught her hand and pulled her to him, his eyes holding hers. She was wearing one of what he thought of as her 'business outfits', a grey suit with a pearl-coloured blouse under it. Her hair was drawn back from her face and he lifted a hand to free it, sending it cascading onto her shoulders. He gave a small sigh of satisfaction as he let it run through his fingers, like molten copper across his palm. Then his shoulders suddenly hunched as he bent to give his own kiss.

There was need in his embrace, a deep longing in the lips that so eagerly took hers. Brett knew he ought to hide it, to control it, but he couldn't; he had thought so often of the first time they'd kissed, so much wanted her in his arms again. She didn't resist or try to fight him, and it was only a moment before she responded, her lips moving under his, her arms going round his neck. He pulled her closer and gave a soft groan as he felt her body against the length of his. An agony of desire ran through him as his lips moved to her throat and he smelt the poignant, somehow mysterious and yet feminine scent of her perfume. His loins *ached* with need of her, his breath grew hot and unsteady. He wanted to tell her how much he wanted her, *hungered* for her, but he knew it was too soon, too soon, and that he must somehow control this desperate yearning. Another tremor ran through him as passion deepened, but then Brett lifted his head, his eyes closed, fighting for self-control.

He was gripping her shoulders, not knowing that his grip was so fierce it was hurting her. Tasha looked up, her own breath unsteady, that startled look again in her eyes. Slowly she reached up and stroked her fingers down his face. Brett gave a shuddering gasp and opened his eyes to look down at her. Harshly he said, 'Do you like to play games with men, to tease them?'

'Do you think I'm teasing you?'

'Yes!' The word was bitten out on a stark note.

'But I'm not.'

Brett looked down at her, not knowing how to take that. 'Why didn't you answer my calls?' he demanded.

She hesitated for a moment and would have moved away, but he wouldn't let her, his grip on her shoulders tightening. 'No, look at me. Tell me.'

Again she hesitated but then said slowly, 'I've been seeing someone.' This time the agony that went through him was one of terrible despair. Brett felt as if the world had suddenly come to an end and he could see no future. 'I had to tell him that it was over before I…'

'Before?' He hardly dared to breathe.

Tasha flushed a little. 'Before I was free to see anyone else.'

It was as if someone had turned on a brilliant light after complete darkness and the world was suddenly wonderful again. Lifting her off her feet, he swung her round, laughing up at her.

'Hey!' She pretended to be indignant. 'Not so much of the macho stuff.'

Brett set her down again but kissed her as he did so, then looked down at her, very much afraid that he was grinning like an idiot.

'What makes you so sure you're the one I want to see?' she asked him dampeningly, but her eyes were laughing.

'What makes you so sure I'd want to see you after you ignored my calls?' he countered.

With a small shrug of her left shoulder, Tasha said simply, 'You're here.' She moved away from him. 'Would you like some wine? There's a bottle of Chardonnay in the fridge.'

'That would be fine.'

He followed her to the kitchen and leaned on the doorframe as he watched her, trying to be nonchalant but feeling his blood still pumping with gratified pleasure and excitement. She fancied him! Liked him enough to ditch her current boyfriend. The fact that she'd done so surprised him; most of the girls he knew wouldn't have bothered, would have thought nothing of dating more than one man at a time. Unless it had been a serious relationship, of course. He thought about that as she reached up to a cupboard to get a couple of glasses and he saw the material of her clothes taut against her body, her slim thighs and rounded breasts. He wanted her all over again and at the same time felt a surge of jealousy about the man she'd been seeing.

But his face betrayed none of his feelings as Brett took the glass she held out to him. 'Should we drink a toast?' he asked, wondering if words could mark this—for him—momentous moment.

'I'm no good at toasts.' Tasha walked ahead of him back into the sitting-room and dropped onto the settee. 'You're the writer; you suggest one.'

'But I only write fiction.'

Tasha liked that. He came to sit beside her and she clinked her glass against his.

He took a sip of wine, then asked, 'What day is it?'

'Friday.'

He took another drink. 'And the date?'

'The twenty-fourth,' Tasha told him, her mouth curving in amusement.

Brett drank again. 'The month?'

'May.' She watched him put the glass to his lips for the fourth time and said, 'Did you just propose a toast without me knowing about it?'

'You could always drink to it yourself.'

'So I could.' For a moment she toyed with the glass as if making up her mind, teasing him a little, but then she raised it and said, 'To today—the twenty-fourth of May.' And she took a long drink, the wine cold and luxurious against her throat.

'A very special day,' Brett murmured and bent to kiss her again. He could taste the wine on her lips, felt first its coldness but then through it the warmth of her mouth. She tasted so good, so sweet. 'I began to get worried when you didn't answer my calls,' he admitted ruefully.

'Good. It doesn't do a man any harm to feel insecure.'

'I'm beginning to think you have a sadistic streak in you.'

He said it playfully but Tasha put her head on one side, considering the idea seriously. Her eyes shadowed. 'Maybe that's necessary sometimes. Especially for a woman.'

'In a love affair, do you mean? When you want to call a halt?' Desperately curious, he was guessing, perhaps probing, although he knew it was unwise to do so.

Her clear, beautiful eyes regarded him steadily, reading his mind. 'Perhaps. And are you cruel?'

'I hope not. I try not to be.' He could have told her that he'd seen too much cruelty in his years as a journalist, but he didn't want to spoil this enchanted moment.

She nodded slowly, apparently believing him, then, in one of her sudden changes of mood, finished her drink and stood up. 'I hope you're going to take me out to dinner, because I'm hungry.'

He would have liked to stay there to eat, but said immediately, 'Of course.'

'Then I'll go and change. Make yourself at home.'

'Are you going to wear that red dress?' he asked.

Tasha paused in the doorway and looked back at

him. Again she gave that Mona Lisa smile as she shook her head. 'No. I think I'll save that for—a special occasion.'

The words held a wealth of promise, the last few spoken in a voice that was even huskier and more seductive than usual. It sent a frisson of excited anticipation running through his veins, and Brett thought that he'd never before met such a tantalising woman. He wondered why on earth she wasn't already married, hadn't been snapped up long ago, and the next moment *really* wondered what the reason was. But then, for all he knew she could have been married, maybe even still was. Was the guy she'd said she'd just ditched her husband? All sorts of ideas went chasing through his mind. She just had to be too good to be true. With that hair and that figure.

Almost angrily he pushed the wild theories out of his mind. He was strongly tempted, while she was changing, to go to her work-room again to have another look at that folder. But maybe he didn't have to go as far as the work-room; Tasha had been carrying a briefcase when she'd arrived home and had dropped it on the floor by the door. He picked it up but it was locked, and it was the kind that needed a combination number to open it. Returning it to its former place, Brett refilled his glass and went to the window, looking out absently, his thoughts running free and all on Tasha as he waited for her.

She was worth the wait. She wore green. A very pale leaf-green dress that left her shoulders and arms bare, fitted to the hips and then swung free. Her hair hung loose as he liked it and she looked altogether delectable. 'You look...' He sought the right words.

'I hope I look half-starved and you can't wait to feed me,' Tasha interrupted before he could find them.

He gave a wry smile, wondering when, if ever, she would allow him to say how he felt about her. 'Do we walk or ride? I'm not too familiar with the restaurants around here.'

'Do you like Thai food? There's a place not too far away.'

'Sounds fine.'

Tasha picked up her bag and a gossamer stole from the hall and they walked to the restaurant. It wasn't the first they passed and Brett couldn't help wondering if she was deliberately avoiding the nearer ones because she was known there, had visited them with her ex-boyfriend. Ex-lover? Ex-husband? He *had* to find out.

But once they were settled in the restaurant Tasha showed no inclination to talk of personal things. She asked him if he'd seen a programme that had been on the television that week, a half-hour piece on artists who painted pictures to illustrate magazine stories and book covers, and the models they used.

Brett shook his head. 'No, I didn't see it. Why, were you involved?'

'Yes, it was my idea and I did all the research,' Tasha told him with evident satisfaction.

'Did you video the programme? I'd like to see it.'

'I have it at home. I'll put it on for you later, if you like.'

So she wanted him to go back with her. Brett had to look away to hide the glint of satisfaction in his eyes. Such an invitation could only mean that she was ready to go to bed with him, wanted it as much as he did. He reached across the table to take her hand and she let him hold it for a minute, but then drew it away as the waiter came up with a bottle of wine.

'What's the name of your company?' Brett asked.

'Plenitude Productions. You probably haven't heard of them, but over the last couple of years we've really started to make a name for ourselves.' She listed some of the programmes the company had made. 'Did you see any of those?'

'Yes, I did. Were you involved with them all?'

'Most of them.'

'I'm impressed. They were memorable.'

Tasha smiled with pleasure and he saw, with no little surprise, that he had found the way to please her. Personal compliments, about her looks, her figure, her hair, she disregarded them all, possibly even resented them, but praise her work and a delightful flush came into her cheeks and her eyes smiled warmly at him. 'Tell me about your work,' he invited. 'How did you get started? Were you a journalist?'

Immediately a shadow came over her face. 'Definitely not. No, I was working in an office, but I had a few ideas which I sent to various production companies. Some of them were accepted so I built up a portfolio of my work. Then I heard that Plenitude were starting up so I went along to see them. I sort of talked my way in to see the boss,' Tasha admitted with an impish grin. 'He liked some of my ideas, put a couple into production, and then offered me a full-time job.'

Brett could imagine her talking her way in; in fact he doubted any man's ability to withstand her when she was really persuasive, when she definitely wanted something. Or any woman's, if it came to that, he thought, remembering the interviews she was currently doing. 'How long ago was that?'

'Nearly three years.'

'Have you thought about going freelance?'

'I did think about it before I joined Plenitude, but the money side of it would have been a bit risky.' She gave a small grimace. 'The rent always has to be paid.'

'I suppose you could always have shared the flat,' Brett suggested, subtly probing.

Her eyes met his in that candid way she had and he guessed she was reading his mind. 'I don't like to share.'

'Never?' There was more behind the question than a simple query.

'No, not in any circumstances.'

The words were spoken in a definite tone that made him wonder why, but their food came and they talked about Thailand, which Brett had visited once, until he remembered another firm answer she'd given him and said, 'Why so definite about not being a journalist?' His eyes were on her face although he kept his voice casual. 'Have you got something against journalism?'

'Not journalism as such. Just journalists, and the way they go about getting their information.'

Carefully, he said, 'You sound as if you speak from experience.'

'Yes, I do. A so-called journalist did the dirty on me once, pinched one of my ideas and sold it to a paper as if it was his own. And as I'd already sold the idea to a television company I wasn't very popular. I had to give them their money back and they didn't employ me again. And—' She stopped abruptly and didn't go on, although he waited.

'Nasty,' Brett said at length. 'But not all journalists are the same, of course.'

'Aren't they?' Tasha frowned, then said on a bitter note, 'I can't think of any I've ever met that I'd trust. All they care about is the story, and they don't care how they have to lie and cheat to get it.'

Thankfully the waiter came up to ask if they were enjoying their meal, and Brett was able to hide the consternation he felt and afterwards change to a safer subject.

He was a good conversationalist and set out to amuse and entertain her, not monopolising things, but inviting her to take part too. Tasha quite enjoyed just listening to him, he had a strong but not obtrusive voice, a voice that went with his character and body, she thought fancifully. Sometimes he would glance away, often when he paused, but most of the time he kept his eyes on her as he spoke instead of looking at a point past her ear as some men did. Somewhat to her own surprise, Tasha had found that she'd missed him during the last few days, had found herself wondering about him, what he was doing. And she'd felt a surge of pleasure when he hadn't been put off by her ignoring his calls and had taken the trouble to find her again.

They finished their meal and lingered over coffee. Picking up her left hand, Brett traced the paler coloured band of skin on her middle finger, the mark left by a ring that had been worn for a long time. 'Did you give it back when you broke it off?' he asked.

Tasha smiled slightly, guessing what he wanted to

know but continuing to tease him a little. 'No, I lost it, quite recently. It flew off my hand when I was taking a ride on a roller-coaster.'

'Big kid,' he said with a grin. Then added, 'And it wasn't on your engagement finger.'

'No, I don't believe in engagements. Do you?'

He shrugged. 'I haven't really thought about it—or tried it. Maybe you're right; maybe they are a bit dated.' He gave a sudden wry smile. 'Let's get all these questions we're wondering about out of the way, shall we? I've never been married, or engaged. How about you?'

'No, nor have I.' Tasha smiled a little. 'But the questions aren't really answered, are they? A denial of total commitment doesn't mean that you haven't had a close relationship, even a whole string of close relationships. That's pretty commonplace nowadays.'

Trying to keep disappointment out of his voice, Brett said, 'And have you had a whole string of close relationships?'

'I meant you.'

'Did you, indeed? What makes you think I fall into that category?'

'How old are you? No—' she held up a hand '—let me guess.' Her eyes studied his face. 'Over thirty. About thirty-three?' He nodded. 'So there are very few men of your age around who haven't had a few affairs in the past.'

'I thought we were talking committed relationships, not affairs.'

'You don't think they're one and the same?'

'No. And I think you know they're not.'

'To a woman they would be,' Tasha said positively.

'Perhaps. To some. But not to a man.'

'So you're saying that men draw a line between sex and emotion.'

Brett grinned. 'Ah, so we're down to the basic differences between men and women already, are we?'

'The battle of the sexes,' Tasha said wryly.

'It doesn't have to be a battle,' Brett pointed out, watching her and wondering what had happened in her past to make her so sardonic.

Glancing up, she caught him studying her and instantly became animated again. 'That was a wonderful meal. Thank you. Let's go, shall we?'

She had shut him out, Brett realised; behind the bright smile, a curtain had been drawn across the window into her character. And she'd also ducked the question of whether she'd ever had a close relationship, he noticed wryly. But maybe she'd open up more when they were in bed together, after they'd made love.

Tasha chatted companionably enough as they strolled back to her flat. She let Brett take her hand and link his fingers through hers and he wondered if she could feel the electric anticipation that filled him. He was a little disappointed not to see any similar feeling in her face. Was she hard? Did she go to bed with so many men that it had become commonplace? He fervently hoped it wasn't like that; he found he very much wanted their lovemaking to be special. When they'd climbed the endless stairs to the flat, Tasha got him a drink and then put on the video she'd told him about.

Kicking off her shoes, she curled up beside him on the sofa and he put his arm round her. Brett tried to concentrate on the programme but found it difficult; he was so consumed with need of her. But he knew the way to please her was through her work so he gave his attention to the screen, wondering if this, again, wasn't some kind of test Tasha was setting him. The documentary was good, he saw that straight away. OK, the subject wasn't that important, but she had researched it thoroughly and had made it not only informative but amusing too. And she'd used actual film footage as much as words to describe the world of magazine story illustrations.

It wasn't that long, and when it was finished he said immediately and sincerely, 'Congratulations. It was a good programme.'

Tasha switched off the set. 'But what did you really think of it—as a writer? And please don't be polite or kind.'

'I wasn't being either. I enjoyed it. You told the story well, without waffling, and you pointed out all the things that an ordinary person wouldn't know and would find interesting. Also, you let the audience see that it could be quite a hard and uncertain life, but the anecdotes you included lightened it when the going could have got heavy. A nicely rounded, entertaining programme. I'm not surprised your boss offered you a full-time job. If I were you I'd ask for a raise in salary.'

'Hey, you don't have to go overboard,' Tasha remonstrated, but there was a flush of pleasure in her cheeks.

'I'm not. Anyway, you don't need me to tell you it was good; you must already know.'

'People have been very kind,' she admitted. 'But as you're a writer I value your opinion.'

Not for the first time Brett saw that his being a writer had made quite an impression on her. He hoped it wasn't only that. He wanted her to fancy him as a man, too. He wanted to glory in her need for him, in her preference for him above all other men. He wanted to make it obvious to other men that she was his, to see the jealousy in their faces as she looked at him with that secret smile a woman had when she was with her lover.

Tasha got up to take the video out of the machine, kneeling on the floor as she put it back in its box. She stayed there, in no hurry, it seemed, to rejoin him on the sofa. After a moment Brett said, 'Have you any more programmes due out?'

She nodded. 'Next month. But it's a programme for teenagers and will be broadcast for schools.'

'And what are you working on now?' He asked the question lightly, but not forgetting for a moment her current project.

She shook her head. 'I told you; it's top secret.' She hugged her knees and added, 'But I have high hopes for it; if I pull it off it could really make my name.'

Or it could do untold damage, Brett thought wryly. He held out his hand. 'Come and sit with me,' he invited.

Tasha hesitated a moment but then came to sit beside him. Her hesitation disturbed him, but the next moment it was forgotten as he put his arms round her and drew her to him.

He kissed her lingeringly, savouring every second,

wanting this night to last. Tasha responded and once again he became lost in the wonder of the embrace, in the intoxication of her closeness. But when his breathing quickened and he lifted his hand to slip the strap of her dress from her shoulder, she moved away from him.

'Tasha?' He said her name on a questioning note, his voice thick with desire.

She didn't speak for a moment but got up and went to the window, stood looking out and then turned to face him. 'Do you want me, Brett?'

'You know I do.'

'You've made—quite an impression on me, too. From the very first.'

'Good. I'm glad.' He got to his feet and would have gone to her, taken her in his arms again, but she held up a hand to stop him. 'What is it?'

'I'm not promiscuous, Brett. There's no way I'd ever go to bed with someone I've known for less than a week.'

She said it so firmly that he felt as if she'd hit him between the eyes. 'You said I'd made an impression on you,' he pointed out.

'You have. I don't think I've ever felt quite like this before—in fact I know I haven't.'

Despite the acute disappointment, he felt immensely pleased and flattered. 'And so?'

'And so I want to get to know you before we—have sex. Anyone can go to bed together, Brett, but I want you for a friend as well as a lover.'

He moved closer and put his hands on her waist, stood looking down at her in the light of the lamps. 'But you do want me?'

Tasha gave a slow smile, said in that gorgeous way she had, 'Absolutely. But I want you—us—to be very, very special.' She put her arms round his neck and said huskily, 'You do understand, don't you?'

'It's going to be very hard.' And he meant it; already his hands ached with the need to hold her body close against his own and let her see how much he hungered for her.

She brushed her lips lightly against his mouth. 'I'll make it up to you—when it's the right time.'

The promise excited him fiercely; his imagination ran riot with pictures of her naked in his arms. She would be wild in bed, he was somehow sure of that, like an exotic flower opening for him—and for him alone. He was suddenly glad that she was going to make him wait, that she didn't go in for one-night stands or have casual relationships. And the fact that she wanted him blew his mind. She was so sensational herself and yet she found *him* special, wanted to know him as a person not just as someone to go to bed with. On a sudden high of emotion he took her in his arms and lifted her off her feet. 'Kiss me,' he commanded.

Laughingly Tasha did so, saying, 'Tarzan has nothing on you.'

He set her on her feet and said, 'OK, we'll wait. But just how long do you think it will take you to get to know me?'

She pretended to consider, head on one side. 'Well, now, you're such a deep character. I should think— at least three months.'

'Three months! I'll die of frustration before then,' he protested in horror.

Tasha laughed delightedly, but then grew serious

again as she said, 'A relationship needs time to grow. And ours is going to be very wonderful. I really feel that.'

Her eyes were so earnest, so beautiful, that Brett felt as if he were drowning in their depths. She made him feel so good, so extraordinarily chosen, that he would have done anything for her at that moment. It even felt completely right that she had refused to go to bed with him. And when he eventually left and walked down the street he still felt elated, as if he was on the verge of the most wonderful experience he had ever known. And it was only later, as he lay alone in his bed, that he realised with a rueful chuckle that he had never before been so skilfully put down in all his life.

CHAPTER THREE

FOR Brett the next few weeks became an entirely new experience in his life. He couldn't remember the last time he had had to take real trouble in pursuing a woman. When he'd fancied someone there might have been a couple of weeks of skirmishing for form's sake, but the conquests had never been difficult or prolonged. There was something about him, perhaps his air of experience and knowledge of their sex, that made a woman know instinctively that he would make a great lover. It was an impression he more than lived up to and he tried to make sure that when an affair inevitably ended they parted as friends.

Not that he'd had a whole string of relationships, as Tasha had suggested; when he'd been younger and fully active as a journalist he had been away a lot, covering the Gulf War, Ireland, wherever there was unrest and the opportunity for a good story. Few chances then to meet the kind of woman he wanted to go to bed with. And with time he'd become even more fastidious, unwilling to have an affair with a woman just because she fancied him; he needed to feel a similar desire. There had been several women he'd been attracted to, of course, and those he'd gone after and—if they were willing—had taken to bed. But no woman had ever fascinated his imagination, had instantly excited his senses, as Tasha had.

He saw her as often as he could but not as often as

he would have liked. Sometimes when they'd arranged a date he would get a call to say that she couldn't make it; she'd been held up at an interview. That, too, was a new experience for him—to be stood up and have to accept it with good grace. But, strangely, that somehow added to the excitement of it. Those highs and lows, expecting to see her and full of anticipation, only to be dashed down and have to spend a lonely evening without her. Often then he wondered who she'd been interviewing and was only saved from intense jealousy by knowing that it had more than likely been a woman.

But Tasha, of course, had no idea that he knew anything about her project, so he'd allowed himself to show some jealousy. One day, after she'd stood him up the previous evening, he'd said, 'Couldn't you have arranged to see this person you were interviewing again some other time?'

'But the interview was going really well,' Tasha said enthusiastically. 'It would have been crazy to stop and try to pick it up again.'

'But we had arranged to go to the theatre,' Brett pointed out, carefully keeping his voice even.

Tasha was immediately contrite. 'I know.' She reached across to touch his hand, her eyes huge. 'And I *did* apologise when I rang. Weren't you able to sell the tickets back? Did they cost the earth?'

He waved that aspect of it away impatiently. 'That doesn't matter. What does matter is that you found your work more interesting than a date with me.'

A slight frown came between her eyes. 'My work is very important to me, Brett.'

He knew it was foolish but he couldn't help saying, 'More important than me?'

She immediately laughed at him. 'What a loaded question! Don't push your luck, mate,' she said, putting on a broad Cockney accent.

Brett grinned, perhaps relieved that she'd lightened the atmosphere. 'And one I can see that you're not going to answer.'

They were perched on high stools in the bar of a restaurant, waiting to be seated. In front of everyone there she reached over and put her hand on his upper leg, then leaned forward and kissed him lingeringly on the mouth. It was the first time she'd ever touched him like that of her own volition in public, or in private if it came to that. Brett gasped against her mouth, a great tremor of suddenly awakened sensuality running through him. Tasha drew her head back a little, her blue eyes laughing at him, dancing with mischief. She went to draw her hand away, but to punish her a little—and because he loved it where it was—he put his own hand over hers and wouldn't let her go.

'Hey!' She raised her eyebrows but was still laughing.

'Kiss me again,' Brett commanded.

'Will I get my hand back?'

'You may never get it back.'

That made her laugh openly and he was rewarded with another kiss, but lightly this time.

Letting her go, Brett glanced round; most of the people in the bar were watching them, the men in open envy. That gave him a great lift, made him feel a million dollars, but he knew, ruefully, that Tasha had evaded him yet again.

He was starting to have difficulty with his own evasions. Tasha didn't pry but she'd shown that she was interested in him, wanted to know him, so how did he account for the years when he'd been a journalist? He wanted to tell her the truth but knew that to do so would be fatal. Not only would she no longer trust him, but she would definitely never tell him about the sexual exploitation theme she was pursuing. So he was trapped and had to come up with a career in an export business that had taken him abroad a lot. Brett didn't like lying, because he could so easily be caught out as much as anything else. They only had to run into someone he knew for the whole thing to blow up in his face. But he felt that he had to take the risk and hope that she would soon care enough about him to confide in him, then he could tell her the truth. Somehow he knew that wouldn't happen until they became lovers, until she gave herself to him.

So he avoided his usual haunts and let Tasha pick where she wanted to go. With the result that he found himself in some bizarre places.

'I'm taking you out tomorrow.' Tasha had called him at one in the morning, when he'd been in bed for an hour. 'Be ready at six and wear old clothes.'

'Do you mean tomorrow as in a few hours, or tomorrow as in after I get another night's sleep?' he asked, looking at his watch.

Tasha sounded surprised. 'In five hours, of course. I'll pick you up. Night.'

'Wait!'

'Yes?'

'That is no way to say goodnight.'

She laughed in that rich, husky tone he loved. 'So what would you like me to say?'

'Can't you think of anything?'

'You want me to flirt with you, right?'

'Yeah. Come on, turn me on.'

'What do you think I am—one of those women you pay to talk sexy over the phone?' She pretended indignation but he could hear amusement in her voice.

'I bet you could do it if you tried.'

'Of course I could—but could you afford the fee?'

'Expensive, huh?'

'Absolutely.'

'I could take out a loan,' he offered.

Tasha laughed again. 'Go to sleep, Brett. See you in the morning.'

Slowly Brett put down the phone, and realised that she hadn't had to talk sexy to him at all; he was already turned on.

She was on his doorstep on the dot of six, pulling up in the yellow sports car, the roof open, and waving to him through it as he looked out of his window. Brett lived in a small house in Docklands. Not one of the new places that had been built in the recent boom years, but a Victorian terraced house in a street that had once housed dockers and their families, people who had been dependent on the work they got from the river but had been forced to move away in search of other work when the dockyards had folded. He had found the house in a half-derelict condition, the roof leaking and windows smashed by vandals, so had got it cheap and repaired the place himself, building on a new kitchen at the back, with a bathroom above it. The house was as good as finished now,

although he still spent time on it when the writing
wouldn't flow.

He ran out to her and got in the car. Tasha looked
wide awake and full of life; anyone would think she'd
had a dozen hours' sleep last night. Her hair was
woven into a thick plait tied with a green ribbon and
she was wearing hardly any make-up. He kissed her
and she smelt gorgeous, of flowers and scrubbed-
clean freshness.

'Where are we going?' he demanded, taking in her
jeans and pale blue shirt.

'It's a surprise.'

'I hate surprises,' he declared untruthfully.

'You'll love this one.'

Brett had imagined a host of things but never that
she would take him fishing. But not just any common
or garden fishing. Not Tasha. She drove him down to
the country to a lake where a friend of hers was waiting for them. He was a middle-aged man who, it
turned out, had once appeared in one of Tasha's television programmes and had become a friend. He
walked to a boathouse with them and pointed. 'There
she is.'

'She' was a canoe, the large version that held two
people and which the man told them had been made
by Canadian Indians. 'I used it a lot when I was out
in Canada for a few years, and brought it back with
me,' he explained.

Brett eyed the frail craft in disbelief. The owner
was only about five feet six and skinny, but Tasha
obviously expected him, Brett, with his six feet two
frame, to get in the thing!

'You don't really expect me to get in that piece of plywood, do you?'

'Mounties use them all the time,' she pointed out.

'That was a hundred years ago—I doubt if they even use horses now; they're probably all trained helicopter pilots.'

'Stop arguing, King; anyone would think you were afraid.'

'I just don't feel like drowning today, Briant, that's all.'

Gingerly he lowered himself into the canoe and sat on the stern seat, then hung on as it rocked dangerously when Tasha blithely jumped in to join him. Brett quite expected it to sink and marvelled when the thing floated with them inside it. The owner, grinning hugely, handed down a couple of fishing rods and a picnic hamper. He watched them as Brett paddled out into the centre of the lake and they took out their fishing rods, then walked off and left them alone.

It was a large lake, the banks mostly overhung by trees, and with a small island in its centre. Brett had done some sailing, which helped, but he found keeping his balance while trying to hook a fish more than a little difficult. When he got a bite he leaned forward eagerly and nearly ended up in the river, just managing to right himself but dropping his rod in the water and getting very wet retrieving it. Tasha, of course, laughed at him, then pretended to ogle him when he took off his shirt to let it dry in the sun, knowing full well she was safe from him.

'Mmm, dig those pectorals,' she enthused. 'I had no idea you had anything so gorgeous tucked away under that shirt.'

He made a face and scooping up a handful of water splashed it over her. 'Now you take yours off to dry and let's see what gorgeous things you've got hidden away under your shirt.'

'Cheat!' She leaned back so that her breasts stretched the wet material, knowing it would tantalise him. 'I think I'll just let the heat of my body dry it.'

His mouth dry, Brett said, 'Vixen.'

Brett enjoyed that day enormously: the gentle lapping of the water, the sun and the peaceful countryside; it was a long time since he'd done that kind of thing and it made him feel young and content. Or almost content. Tasha was tormentingly close enough to see but not to touch, so he let his line become entangled with hers so they had to move close together to untangle them.

'You did that on purpose!'

'Of course. I want to kiss you.'

'If you do we'll both end up in the lake.'

'I'll chance it.' Reaching out, he held her as he kissed her, but when he tried to pull her close the boat rocked alarmingly and he had to hastily let go. 'You are driving me mad with frustration,' he told her. 'Come home with me tonight.'

'All right.'

He nearly upset the boat in surprise. 'You will?'

'Yes, I haven't seen your place yet.'

Brett managed to catch a couple of decent-sized fish, and in the late afternoon they paddled over to the island and built a fire on which they cooked them, eating them between hunks of bread and washed down with beer. Afterwards Brett leaned back against the trunk of a tree and Tasha sat beside him. Her thoughts on Canada, she began to sing 'Rose Marie' in a clear, sweet voice, and made him join in, the sound drifting across the lake. When the last note had died away he pulled her closer to rest against him and nuzzled her neck as they watched the sun set into rich golds and purples, the flaming colours made doubly beautiful by their reflection in the water. Tasha smiled, gave a long sigh, then turned her head and let him kiss her.

'We must do this again,' he said, meaning it.

She smiled in delight. 'I knew you'd enjoy my surprise.'

They paddled back to the jetty, leaving the canoe securely tied, and drove unhurriedly back to London, to Brett's house.

Tasha wanted to see everything, to hear about the restoration work he'd done and see all his before and after photos of the place. Her interest was gratifying but he was on tenterhooks; it was only a month since they'd met and she'd said it had to be at least three months before she'd let him make love to her. But had she changed her mind? Was she sure enough of him, of her own feelings to...?

Brett found himself clenching his fists in hope and fear of disappointment.

In the sitting-room he had a huge settee that nearly filled the room, even bigger than the one Tasha had in her flat. He put on a CD and got drinks and she snuggled up to him like a child. They talked about the day for a while but then he kissed her longingly. Tasha put her drink aside, put her arms round his neck and sent his senses reeling as she returned the kiss more ardently than ever before. And this time, when his fingers began to undo the buttons of her shirt, she didn't stop him.

Her breasts were beautiful; not full enough to fill his unsteady hands but soft and rounded, the pale pink nipples at first unawakened but then hardening delightfully as he gently caressed them with his fingertips. They tilted pertly at him then, and he was unable to resist bending his head to gently take them each in turn into his mouth, to toy with them, kiss them, caress them with his tongue. Satisfied at last, his lips moved on to trail across her shoulders and kiss her neck. Tasha sighed and lifted her head, squirmed deliciously as he bit her earlobe, and whispered his name as he took her mouth at last.

By now his senses were on fire, but Brett kept them banked; it was early yet and he fully intended to make love to her all night, so there was time to linger, to lengthen each moment, to enjoy each new discovery to the full. Tasha returned his kiss, her hands with a delicate fingertip touch on each side of his face. Her kiss was warm, tender, responsive, but that was all. The passion had died, there was no eager searching, no hunger. At first he thought that she, too, was holding desire in check, but then recognised her kiss for what it was: participation but not encouragement. Raising his head, Brett looked at her questioningly.

'That was nice.' She smiled at him—and reached for her clothes.

'"Nice?"' For a moment he was angry and, reaching out, caught her wrist. 'Is that all? Just "nice"?'

She became still, her eyes fixed on his face. 'You know the terms, Brett.'

'Damn it, I thought—' He broke off, biting his lip.

'Does there have to be terms? Does there have to be a time limit?'

Tasha looked away from him for a moment, then lifted her head to look steadily into his eyes. 'Yes, I'm sorry, but there does.' Drawing her wrist from his hold, she reached for her bra and put it on, covering up all the loveliness that he thought had been his.

Getting to his feet, Brett strode over to the sideboard and poured himself a drink, his hand shaking. 'Do you make a habit of this?' he demanded, desperately trying to control his disappointment.

'Of what?'

'You know damn well what! Of leading a man on and then slapping him down.' He turned and saw that she was completely dressed and standing up, her hands thrust into the pockets of her jeans.

'You think it unfair, do you?'

'Yes, of course I do.'

She grew suddenly angry. 'And do you think it fair to kiss me and caress me and turn me on when you know that I want to wait?'

He stared at her in surprise. 'But that must mean that…'

'That I want you? Yes, of course it does. Did it never occur to you that I might want you as much as you want me? I told you that you were special!'

Putting down his glass, Brett strode over and took hold of her arms, desperate pleading in his face. 'In that case what is there to wait for? I *ache* for you, Tasha. I long to—'

'*No!*' She pushed him angrily away. 'Why won't you listen to me? All you're thinking of is yourself.

I have to be sure. I couldn't bear to be hurt again. Now do you understand?'

'You mean someone in the past...?'

'Yes.'

'Who? What happened?'

'You have no right to ask me that question. You don't know me well enough to ask it. I don't ask you about the women in your past.'

'That's different. A man—'

'No, it damn well isn't! Men always assume they have the right to know everything about a woman. Well, they don't. And you have no right to assume that I'll go back on my terms just because you want me to. When I give myself to you it will be when I'm good and ready, and not before.' Her eyes flashed fire at him as she drew herself up defiantly. 'And if you can't handle that, then you don't have to stick around!'

Brett stared, completely taken aback. For a blinding moment he saw a future when she was no longer a part of his life, when he didn't spend all his time looking forward to seeing her again, thinking about her and longing to make love to her, a time of not having this agonisingly familiar ache for her deep inside. It was unthinkable. His mind refused to accept it, even to envisage it. 'Don't say that!' His hands tightened convulsively on her arms. 'Don't ever say that again.'

'Then don't try to coerce me. You must take what I'm willing to give.' She gazed at him intently, waiting for his answer, his promise.

Brett gave a long sigh, then straightened up and

relaxed his hold a little. 'You're a strong woman, Tasha.'

She didn't deny it. 'I've learned to be.'

'Tonight—could we do that again from time to time? You know—drive me mad with frustration?'

Her eyes filled with amusement. 'Drive *both* of us mad,' she corrected him.

He nodded. 'Yeah.'

Happy again, she slipped her arms round his neck. 'I think that could be arranged.'

Touching the end of her nose with his, Brett said, 'Will I ever understand you?'

'Perhaps. In time.'

'Time!' He said the word on a raw, wry note.

'We have all the time in the world,' she pointed out.

'I just hope I'm not too old by the time you get round to making up your mind.'

That made her laugh. 'I'll try to make sure you're not.' She moved her hips provocatively against his. 'In fact I'll promise that you'll still be very, very active.'

For a moment he closed his eyes, letting desire rise and then die. 'This has never happened to me before,' he murmured.

'You mean you've never met a girl like me before.'

'You can say that again,' he said with sincerity.

Lifting herself on tiptoe, Tasha kissed him lightly. 'It will be worth it; you know that.'

She left him then but rang when she got home.

'Are you in bed?'

'Yes, but somehow I don't think I'm going to get much sleep tonight.'

'Why not?'

'You know why not; my libido has been seriously damaged. I'm not at all sure it will ever recover.'

'It will! It will! What are you wearing?'

'I don't wear anything in bed.'

'Wow! And do you have silk sheets?'

'Hey! I'm the one who's supposed to ask those sort of questions.'

'This is a free country. What colour are the sheets?'

'Come over and find out.'

'I bet they're black. I bet you have black silk sheets.'

'That's naff.'

'Right. And you're definitely not naff.'

'I'm not?'

'No. You're… But perhaps I'd better not tell you.'

'You're too kind to put me down. Right?'

'Wrong. I just don't want to make you so frustrated that you won't be able to sleep for a week! Goodnight, Brett.'

He liked the way she'd phoned him, and the way the conversation had gone. As he lay in bed thinking about her he decided that he had never met a woman who was so feminine and yet at the same time so independent as Tasha. She seemed to make her own rules. He wondered about the man who had hurt her and felt a fit of angry rage, would have liked to punch his face in. But if she hadn't been hurt would she have become the fascinating woman that she was now? His mind went back to the way she'd let him kiss her tonight and he tossed on his pillow frustratedly. God, he'd never wanted any woman so much in all his life! He tried to tell himself that the world wouldn't come to an end if he didn't get an immediate gratification of his hunger for her, but her resolve—and therefore her ability to control her own needs—made him slightly resentful. How could Tasha possibly want him as badly as he wanted her if she could say no, even threaten to just walk away? Again a feeling of panic at the thought swept over him, and he knew that he would go to any lengths to keep her. *Because he just had to have her.*

'I'm sorry, Miss Briant, but there's nothing I can do until a new lock can be fitted.' It was a week or so later, and Tasha stood in angry frustration at the entrance to her garage. Pranksters had super-glued the lock on the gates that closed off the driveway and none of the tenants could get their cars out. And she'd arranged to meet the employee of a Middle Eastern big-shot this afternoon for what could turn out to be one of the most important interviews for her programme. Darn! The girl was only in England for a couple of days and they'd arranged to meet at the home of her sister, which was half way across the country, and being Sunday it would be impossible to hire a car.

Tasha hesitated for only a moment and then rang Brett's number. Quickly she explained about the car. 'I've got an important appointment and I've just got to have a car,' she told him. 'Can I possibly borrow yours?'

Guessing what kind of appointment she'd have on a Sunday, Brett thought fast and said, 'Of course you're welcome to borrow it, but have you ever driven a four-wheel drive before?'

'Well, no, but surely it's the same as any other car?'

'Not really. And I'm afraid mine's so old that it can be touchy and temperamental if you're not used to it. How about if I drive you where you want to go?'

'That's kind of you, Brett, but I'm sure I'll be able to handle it.'

'Why don't I bring it over and you can try it out?' he offered.

She accepted gratefully and Brett drove across London to a street a couple of blocks from Tasha's place where he stopped and made one or two adjustments to the car. Then he drove on to her building.

Tasha ran to meet him and gave him a hug. 'This is brilliant of you.'

'Try it first,' he cautioned.

She got in the driver's seat, confident of her ability to handle the vehicle, but listened patiently while Brett ran through its idiosyncrasies. There seemed to be an awful lot of them. He insisted on sitting beside her while she tried it out. She started off and within seconds was exclaiming in horror, 'This steering is all over the place!' She tried to stop but the brake pedal went down to the floor without anything happening. And they were coming up to a busy junction with the traffic lights against them!

Kicking her foot off the pedal, Brett pumped it and they came to an abrupt stop.

Her eyes wide with horror, Tasha said faintly, 'My God, how on earth can you get around in this thing?'

'I told you it was temperamental.'

'Yes, but you neglected to add that it was a time-bomb on wheels.'

'Perhaps you'd prefer not to use it? Can you borrow a different car?'

Tasha looked down at her watch. 'There isn't time.' She frowned in impatience, then said, 'Can you really drive it safely?'

'Oh, sure, I'm used to it.'

'Then would you take me, please? I can't miss out on this interview.'

'Of course.' They changed places and Brett drove cautiously along. 'Where do you want to go?'

'It's a village called Highclere St Mary's, in Derbyshire.'

'Quite a way, then. I'd better get some petrol.' Stopping at the first service station they came to, he said, 'I don't have a map for that area; do you think you could buy one from the shop?'

Tasha hurried off to get one and, as soon as she was out of sight, Brett lifted up the bonnet of the car and reversed the adjustments he'd made earlier. When she returned he was calmly filling the tank. Afterwards they seemed to make better progress and Brett had no difficulty in handling the car, although he was careful not to let it seem too easy.

'You said you were going to do an interview; is that for the television programme you're working on?'

'Yes.' She was less than informative.

'Don't you have to take a camera crew and all the equipment along when it's television?' Brett asked in what he hoped was a casual query.

Relaxing a little, Tasha said, 'Yes, of course, but at the moment I'm just doing the research—working out who to include in the actual programme and who to leave out. Some people might not even want to appear, although they're willing to contribute.'

'What do you do in that case? Black them out or hide their faces or something?'

'Yes, or we can use just their voices over some ordinary film shots. Perhaps of the area they're describing, that kind of thing.'

'It must be fascinating. I'm afraid I know very little about how a television programme is put together.'

Which wasn't completely true, but it gave her an opening and, thankfully, it was one into which Tasha innocently stepped. She described the work involved and told him several really funny stories about the programme she'd made for schools.

She told the stories well, making Brett laugh so much that he coughed and had to take his hand off the wheel while at the same time changing gear. The car didn't veer an inch from the straight. Tasha looked at the steering wheel then raised her eyes to his face. 'You fixed the car, didn't you?'

'I wasn't happy about you driving it yourself,' he admitted. 'So I—er—accentuated the faults a little.'

'I ought to punish you for that.'

He raised a wary eyebrow, but she didn't look as annoyed as he'd expected her to be. 'Yeah?'

'Yeah. And I would if I didn't think that you'd probably enjoy it.'

He laughed at that, relief in his voice, and tried to gain her trust even further by getting her to help him with a snag in the plot of his new book. Brett knew she enjoyed discussing his work with him and hoped that she would do the same with her own work. But he had to ask, 'Is this an important person you're seeing today?' before he got anything at all out of her.

'No, not really. She's just an ordinary kind of woman.'

'And do ordinary women make good television programme material?'

She looked at him for a moment but he kept his eyes on the road. 'Only when they've had something—out of the ordinary happen to them,' she said after a long moment.

'Such as?'

But she wouldn't tell him and changed the subject. When they found the address she was looking for, Tasha went to get out of the car and said, 'I'm sorry, but I can't take you with me; I promised I'd see her alone.'

'No problem. I'll go and find somewhere to have lunch. You can call me on my mobile when you want me to pick you up.'

He was rewarded with a brilliant smile. 'I really appreciate this, Brett.'

Raising a suggestive eyebrow, he gave her a wink and said, 'It might cost you later.'

Although he had said it in fun it had been the wrong thing to say, and she didn't smile. 'I hope you don't mean that.'

Leaning across, he kissed her lightly. 'Your terms,' he reminded her.

Her eyes grew warm and she put her hand on his cheek as she kissed him back, her mouth open, sensuous, immediately arousing desire. Lifting her head, she opened languid eyes that smiled into his, making him feel as if he were the only man in the world. 'See you later.' And then she was gone, running up the driveway to the house and lost to his sight. Brett sat there for a long moment, wondering why no other woman had ever had the ability to make him feel so special before, then slowly drove away.

The girl Tasha had come to see worked as a stewardess for a man who had his own private jet. He was immensely rich and paid very well, but he expected a great deal for his money. 'I had to send a full-length photo before I even went for the interview,' the woman, Anne, told Tasha. 'And when I got the job I had to sign a two-year contract. I thought that being from the Middle East he would want me to wear discreet, if not demure clothes, but the owner chose the uniform himself and it had a very short skirt. Well, OK, I've got good legs, and I wear short skirts all the time at home, so it didn't worry me too much. But then he made it clear that there were other "services" he wanted while he was on the plane, besides serving him meals.'

'What did you do?' Tasha asked, fascinated.

'I refused. I decided to quit as soon as I could get another job, and I told him so. But he said that I'd never get another job, that he'd make it his business to see that my name was blackened with every airline I applied to. On the other hand, he said he would make it well worth my while to do as he wanted. He offered me a really luxurious apartment in the capital of his country and promised me a huge bonus when my two years were up.'

'Couldn't you get any other kind of a job here in England?'

'Only as a waitress or something similar, and even

those jobs aren't that easy to find—especially if you need to live in, as I did. And besides, he took away my passport; he said he kept all his staff passports together.'

'Can he do that?'

Anne shrugged. 'When you have that much money you also have unlimited power; you can do what you damn well like. It didn't matter at first because when I got the flying job I was over the moon, until he made it plain he wanted to join the Mile-High Club.'

'What on earth is that?'

'You haven't heard of it? It's a very select membership. You can only join if you've had sex when you're at least a mile up in the sky.'

'Wow!'

'He has part of the plane fitted out as a bedroom. I have to make myself available during every flight.' Anne gave a short laugh. 'And I save a bomb on underwear because I'm not allowed to wear any under my uniform.' The two girls gazed at each other for a moment, then Anne looked away from the growing anger in Tasha's face. 'He gives me presents,' she said. 'Jewellery, that kind of thing. And with the bonus he promised me I'd have enough to live on for a long time if I was careful.'

'How long have you been working for him?'

'Twenty months.'

'So you'll soon be free of him.'

'Yes.' But Anne gave her a haunted look.

'What is it? Why have you decided to tell me all this?'

Anne hesitated a moment, then said, 'Sometimes he has guests on the plane, other men. He knows my two year contract is nearly up, and he's told me that unless I do for these other men what I do for him, and—and let him watch, then I'll have broken the conditions of the contract and I won't get a penny.'

'The louse!' Tasha exploded. 'The filthy rat.'

She was still furiously angry when she called Brett and he came to collect her. He was about to ask her how the interview had gone, but took one look at her face and changed his mind.

Tasha was seething, her hands clenched in her lap. They had gone only about a mile when she could stand it no longer. 'For God's sake stop this car.'

Luckily it was an open, minor road and Brett was able to immediately swerve into the side and pull up just near the entrance to a field. Jumping out, Tasha ran to the five-barred gate into the field, pushed it open and began to storm up and down, muttering furiously.

Following her, Brett said, 'What is it? What did you say?'

'Men!' She swung round on him. 'They should all be castrated at birth.'

He stared in shocked amazement. 'Are you including me in that statement?'

'You're a man, aren't you?'

'Now hold on there.' He went to take hold of her arm but she hit out at him. Angry, he grabbed her shoulders and shook her. 'Tasha!'

She glared at him for a moment, then suddenly slumped, and he saw that she had tears in her eyes. 'It's so unfair, so cruel. The way men use women, coerce them, humiliate them. God, it makes me so darn mad.' She pushed herself away and stood with her back to him, her arms crossed, hugging herself in distress.

Seeing that the anger went too deep to be just on behalf of the unknown woman that she'd interviewed, Brett went to stand behind her and gently rubbed her arms. 'Tell me,' he said softly.

'I can't. I promised her I wouldn't.'

'You're not thinking about her, you're thinking about yourself.'

She became very still, then slowly turned to face him.

Her beautiful eyes were smudged with tears and he felt a great surge of emotion, as if someone had kicked him in the stomach. 'Oh, Tasha.' He opened his arms and she stood for a moment, then came to lean her head against his chest. Stroking her back, he said inadequately, 'It's OK, you're all right.'

Sighing, she said, 'Sometimes the world is a bloody rotten place.'

Brett kissed her hair and said, 'Don't worry, I'll take care of you.'

She laughed on a sardonic note, straightened up out of his hold and pushed her hair off her face. 'I don't need a *man* to take care of me. I can look after myself.'

Annoyed that she'd included him in a category she obviously despised, he said, 'Oh, sure. You know what you remind me of, Tasha? One of those chocolates that's hard on the outside, but when you bite into it the centre is so soft it just melts away.'

'I admit that I get angry when I hear of a woman who's being ill-used,' she admitted tightly.

'And do you think women don't ill-use men? Of

course they do. Some of them. Just like it's only some men who mistreat women. You can't just lump them all together, Tasha.'

She gazed at him for a moment, then turned and walked away, stooping to pick a long stalk of grass which she began to pull to pieces. 'Sometimes I think that men are born knowing how to abuse women.' He didn't answer and, her head lowered, she went on, 'I left school at eighteen and went straight to college. There was a lecturer there, a middle-aged married man. He was my course tutor and I often had to see him alone. He made a pass at me, and when I resisted he said that if I didn't do as he wanted he'd make sure I failed my exams. So I told him that if he didn't keep away from me I'd report him to the college authorities.'

Her voice faltered. 'Then one day—one beautifully sunny afternoon—he tried to rape me. He did it quite deliberately, holding a cushion over my head so I couldn't scream. He half suffocated me, but I'd had some training in self-defence and I managed to get him off. I raked his face with my nails and kicked him where it hurts most. Then I left him and ran, but when I complained to the college authorities they wouldn't believe me. The tutor was a respectably married man with grown-up children. He was a grandfather, for God's sake. So who the hell do you think they believed?' She gave a harsh, brittle laugh. 'They said it would be better all round if I just left the college quietly.'

Consumed with the deepest rage, Brett said harshly, 'Who is he? Just tell me who he is.'

A small smile creased her mouth and he saw deep

satisfaction in her eyes. 'Oh, you don't have to worry; I made sure he'd never misuse another student long ago.'

Brett stared at her, wild ideas chasing through his mind. 'What did you do?'

'Oh, nothing melodramatic. I went straight to the Rape Crisis Centre in the town and told them about it. It seemed I wasn't the first who had complained about him, but I was the first who was willing to give evidence in a trial. They took up the case and forced the college to listen. He tried to say that I had seduced him, that I was willing, but he had the scratches on his face. So he was eventually made to leave. But it was all hushed up, of course,' she added bitterly.

'So you went back to university?'

Tasha laughed again. 'You're joking! I got kicked out before I'd even been there a whole term. The principal tried to buy me off. He said I could stay on at the college if I would drop the charges against the lecturer. When I refused, there was no chance of going back, to that or any other college. It's like a men-only club; they all stick together, try to protect their own. But at least his reputation was ruined, and will be even more so when my television programme is shown.'

Brett's face tightened as he took in the implications. 'Can you do that? Haven't you had revenge enough?'

She looked him steadily in the eyes. 'He ruined my life and that of several other girls. Do you really think it fair? After what he did to me it was a long time before I could even be alone in a room with a man. There were times when I didn't want to live, knowing that people were looking at me, talking.' She put on a gossipy voice. '"She must have asked for it. I bet she flaunted herself until he couldn't resist." That's the kind of thing they said. And besides—' her eyes hardened '—there were a lot of girls, some of them married women, who wouldn't give evidence but who had suffered at his hands over the years. And most of them had taken the easy way out, had been forced to do what he wanted. They, too, need to be avenged.'

Brett gave a long, low whistle. Then, able to open up the subject himself at last, he said, 'So what is this programme going to be about? The way men use women?'

Tasha hesitated, a rueful look coming into her eyes as she realised she'd given herself away. Briefly she nodded. 'Yes.' She gave him a challenging look. 'Do you have any problem with that?'

Slowly Brett shook his head. 'I don't, no. But I can see that you might have problems, Tasha. Very big problems.'

CHAPTER FOUR

'I DON'T want to talk about it.' Striding past him, Tasha headed for the car.

Brett didn't push it. He felt that he'd made some progress, even though Tasha had given him the information inadvertently. But he would have to go carefully, show no undue curiosity, or she would shut up like the proverbial clam.

So as they drove back to London he talked of other things, but when he saw that Tasha wasn't listening, was sitting with a brooding look on her face, he switched on a music channel on the radio and drove the rest of the way in silence. When they reached her flat he made sure he got out of the car with her. Tasha hesitated for a moment, wanting to work on the notes she'd taken of the interview, but then smiled and said, 'Are you hungry? I could make an omelette or something.'

'Sounds great.'

Being on the top floor, the rooms felt hot and stuffy. Tasha pushed open all the windows, letting in what breeze there was, and the noise of traffic from the streets below. They ate and he helped her wash up, then settled on her sofa with a cool drink.

'It was nice to get out into the country for a while,' Brett remarked. 'I went for a walk while I was waiting for you; I think I'd almost forgotten what the countryside smelt like.'

Tasha smiled. 'Cow-pats and pigsties.'

'Manure heaps and mangel-wurzels,' he agreed with a grin.

'What on earth are mangel-wurzels?'

'I haven't the faintest idea, but they are definitely very countrified.'

'You're more likely to find farmers breeding llamas and ostriches than cows and sheep nowadays,' Tasha said prosaically.

'Possibly.' He stroked the back of her hand with his finger. 'Personally I prefer the sound of seagulls to that of rooks cawing, and the smell of the ocean rather than manure heaps. And I like to walk for miles along the open beach instead of hopping over gates and stiles to cross fields.'

'Are you getting nostalgic for your cottage in Cornwall?'

'I think I must be.'

'But there's a lot going on in London. The summer festival starts soon. There'll be jazz concerts in the parks.'

'And in Cornwall the deep lanes will be like cloisters, overhung with trees, and the banks heavy with flowers and blossom.'

'And nose to tail with cars. And the beaches crowded with tourists.'

'Not in my cove,' he said positively.

'Your cove! Hark at the man.'

His hand closed over hers. 'If I go to Cornwall, will you come with me?'

Turning her head, Tasha studied his face. 'As a friend?'

'Yes—and as a lover.'

'As your mistress.' There was a faintly disparaging note in her voice.

'No. As a lover. An equal partner in a wonderful experience.'

She gave a small smile. 'Will it be wonderful?'

'Oh, yes,' he said with sincerity. 'I guarantee it.'

She hesitated a moment, then said, 'When are you going and for how long?'

Hope soared. 'As soon as you like and for as long as you like.'

'It would be nice to get out of London for a while,' Tasha said on a wistful note. 'But I'm so busy with my programme.'

'You could spare a few days.'

She smiled, her eyes on his face. 'Could I?'

'Mmm.' She had this knack of studying him with such warmth in her eyes that it was like a caress. And with that little teasing smile on her lips so that he was never sure what she was thinking. 'Would you like a preview?'

Her brows rose. 'Of what it would be like at your cottage?'

'Of what we would do there, yes.'

Her gaze grew very innocent. 'You mean walking on the beach, and that kind of thing?'

'No, I meant lying on the bed—and that kind of thing.'

'Oh!' She pretended to understand. Then filled him with delighted surprise when she added, 'You mean this.' And, pushing him back on the settee, she kissed him and began to undo his shirt.

Her hands roved delicately over him, so cool against his suddenly over-heated skin. She explored freely, caressing his tiny nipples, curling the hairs on his chest round her fingers. He loved every second of it and squirmed when she found that he was ticklish. Tasha laughed. 'So I've found your weak spot, have I?'

'I'm afraid I have a great many weak spots where you're concerned.'

'Really? And is this another one?' She was half lying over him and lowered herself a little so that she could kiss his neck, the line of his strong jaw, the minute cleft in his chin. Brett stood that easily enough but then she moved on down and her tongue trailed across his chest until it found his nipple. He groaned then and clumsily reached to pull off her blouse, but she lifted her head and said huskily, 'No, this is just for you.'

So he lay back and let her caress him, his senses burning, on fire, his skin trembling where she touched him, kissed him. His body was fiercely aroused and his fingers dug into her hips as he held her. Tremor after tremor of awareness ran through him, and he groaned as she gently bit him. To have her kiss him, toy with him like this, when he knew that she wouldn't let him touch her in return or let him make love to her, was an exquisite torture. Overwhelming pleasure mixed with the most terrible sexual frustration. He felt like a toy, a plaything, an inanimate object that longed to spring to life.

At last she lifted herself and kissed his mouth. Brett grabbed her and held her head as he kissed her passionately in return. 'Come to Cornwall,' he said against her mouth. 'Oh, God, you've got to come.

You're driving me mad. Crazy! I want you so much, *so much.*'

Lifting her head, Tasha looked at his lean, hungry face. 'All right.'

He hugged her in exuberant joy and relief. 'When?'
'Soon.'

Beyond that she wouldn't go; he could get no definite date out of her. And soon she stood up and said pointedly, 'Would you like another drink before you go?'

Brett groaned. 'Are you throwing me out?'

'I want to write up the notes on my interview while it's still fresh in my mind. Decide how I'm going to handle it.'

He sighed, stood up and pulled on his shirt. 'Will I see you tomorrow?'

'No, I have a date.'

'Male or female?'

Tasha smiled. 'Do I ask you who you see?'

'No—but I wish you would.'

'Why?'

'Because I want you to be very, very jealous,' Brett said feelingly.

She came and put her arms round his neck, ran her fingers through his hair. 'Have I reason to be jealous?'

For a moment he was tempted to make up a girl-friend, an old flame or something, but then knew that she wouldn't believe him. 'No,' he growled. 'You know darn well you haven't.' He looked at her keenly. 'Have I?'

She moved away from him and her voice was cool as she said, 'I'm seeing an old friend that I used to work with. A *girl*friend. We meet up every couple of months.'

'Will you tell her about me?'

Her mouth twisted in amusement. 'Perhaps.'

'What will you tell her?'

Tasha laughed openly. 'That you're a *man*—but I'm trying to turn you into a civilised human being.'

'Ouch.' He picked up her hand, kissed it, his eyes on her face, then asked a question he knew he shouldn't, but couldn't resist. 'Do you ever run into the man you were seeing before me?'

'No.' She shook her head, but there was a wary look in her eyes.

'Who was he?'

'No one of any importance.'

He frowned. 'Was he ever—important?'

'Goodnight, Brett.'

He saw that she wasn't going to answer him, that he would never know if she'd been to bed with this other man. Provoked, he said, 'I could almost feel sorry for him, if he felt for you as I feel.'

Tasha's voice hardened a little. 'If he wanted me as much as you do, you mean?'

'Yes, I suppose so. Did he?'

She turned away and walked to the door to open it for him, said again, 'Goodnight, Brett.'

Picking up his jacket, he slung it over his shoulder and walked over to her. 'So when will I see you?'

She shrugged. 'I'm pretty busy at the moment.'

He paused, looking into her face, then said softly but with intense feeling, 'Don't punish me because I want you, Tasha. You know it's beyond my control.'

Her eyes softened and she reached up to kiss him.

Holding her afterwards, Brett said, 'You say you want to get to know me, but you tell me so little about yourself. I sometimes feel that I know nothing about you.'

She gave him a contemplative look, then said, 'Are you free on Wednesday. I'll take you out.'

'Where?'

'It's a surprise.'

He gave a mock groan. 'I'm becoming wary of your surprises.'

But on the whole he was greatly pleased with the way the day had gone. Her television project was at last out in the open, even though Tasha had told him little about it. He would be able to talk to her now, try and get her to confide in him even more. He would dearly like to know who she'd seen today and why it had made her so overwhelmingly angry. But he hadn't wasted his time while Tasha had been doing the interview; he'd asked a few casual questions in the village pub and found out the name of the owner of the house. It shouldn't be too difficult to find out the maiden name of his wife, and that should lead to her sister, the woman Tasha had met there. Brett still had plenty of connections in journalism, plenty of experience in ferreting out the information he wanted.

And she had promised to go to Cornwall with him. His spirits soared at the thought of it. There, where they would be entirely alone, she would not only give her body to him, but he would be able to work on her, make her trust him, so that she told him all about the project, all he wanted to know. But his thoughts were mostly filled with the enormous anticipation of making love to her at last, of satisfying this dreadful ache of longing that drove nearly everything else out of his mind.

Tasha's thoughts were on Cornwall, too, as the next day she took a cab to the wine-bar where she'd arranged to meet her friend, Sarah. They hugged, and talked first about Sarah's live-in boyfriend for a while.

'How long has it been now?' Tasha asked.

'Almost two years.'

'And you and Clyde are still happy just living together?'

Sarah hesitated, then said, 'Actually, I wouldn't mind getting married. I feel that we've been together long enough to know that we're really compatible, in every way. And I'd like to start a family.'

'Getting broody?' Tasha said sympathetically.

'I suppose I must be. My sister had a baby not long ago, a little boy, and he's so beautiful, Tasha.'

'What does Clyde say?'

A frown came into Sarah's eyes. 'He thinks there's still plenty of time. And he isn't keen on getting saddled with a huge mortgage for a house. But, like I said to him, I would still be working. Even if we had a baby, I would still go back to work afterwards.'

Tasha studied her face for a moment, noted the obstinate look to Sarah's mouth. 'Maybe it might be better not to push too hard,' she suggested. 'You might grow out of these feelings in a while.'

'I don't think so. And anyway, if he really loved me he'd want to marry me.'

'Maybe he doesn't feel ready yet.'

'What difference would it make? We're as good as married already.'

'So why bother to get married, then?'

Sarah stared at her. 'That's what Clyde says. But I'd like to be married before I have a baby.'

'So work on him gently. Make him think it's a good idea too.'

She tried to persuade her further, and they were on to their food before they got round to talking about Tasha. 'Who are you dating?' Sarah finally asked. 'Is it still the painter?'

'No, someone new. He's a writer.'

Sarah smiled. 'All these artistic types you go for. What's he like?'

'Nice. A bit special.'

'Really? Tell me about him.'

'He's quite good-looking in a tough kind of way. Very self-possessed. Very masculine.'

'And head-over-heels in love with you, I suppose. They usually are.'

'He wants me,' Tasha admitted.

'What man doesn't? But do you want him?'

'Definitely.'

Sarah's eyebrows rose. 'That sounds very decisive. Have you done anything about it?'

'Not yet. It's too soon.'

But Tasha smiled as she said it, her eyes warm, and Sarah gave her a long look. 'Be careful, Tasha, this man sounds as if he could do serious damage.'

Tasha frowned. 'What do you mean?'

'I mean that he could damage your heart—if you let him.'

'I think that might be a risk I'll have to take.' But she smiled again as she said it.

* * *

Brett had no idea what to expect when Tasha took him out on the following Wednesday, but fully expected it to be something energetic. So he was genuinely surprised when she took him to—of all places—the circus. The big top was set up on a huge piece of common land on the outskirts of a town to the north of London, a little apart from a traditional funfair full of stalls and rides: everything from coconut shies to a ghost train. They wandered round these first, Tasha insisting that Brett try his hand at several of the stalls. He did best at the rifle range and won her a prize.

'Wow!' she exclaimed. 'That was brilliant. Where did you learn to shoot?'

It had been while covering a war for a newspaper, but Brett wasn't about to tell her that. 'Sign of a misspent youth,' he said flippantly. 'What prize would you like?' He looked along the shelves lined with white bunnies, cuddly teddies and adorable dogs. 'It looks like a furry animal or a furry animal.'

He fully expected her to pick one of those but instead Tasha pointed to a green frog with a big mouth that wasn't at all appealing. 'I'll have that one.'

As they walked away from the stall he said, 'Why that one?'

Holding up the frog, Tasha looked at it consideringly. 'It reminds me of someone.'

'God, I hope it isn't me!'

That made her laugh. 'Which one do you think should have reminded me of you? A teddy bear? Or perhaps the lion? Or the rabbit?'

He gave her a playful punch on the nose. 'Watch it, Briant.'

'No, tell me—which one?'

'Do you take teddy bears to bed with you?'

So this time she gave *him* a punch on the nose.

They had ringside seats for the circus, and as he sat down Brett saw that they were surrounded by families, most of them with fairly young children. He felt out of place and wondered what the hell they were doing there. He was used to the old-fashioned type of circus with performing animals: lions and tigers in their cage with a loin-clothed trainer, or elephants that could stand on their hind legs. But wild animals were no longer a part of the modern circus and he expected the performance to be flat, bland and unexciting. But the show horses were still there, cantering on in their glittering panoply of plumes and jewelled harness, and soon he found that he was enjoying himself.

The clowns were marvellous and soon had everyone laughing, especially the children. One of them, dressed in a green outfit and with great, white-painted eyes and a wide mouth, seemed to notice them and do most of his antics in their part of the ring. And at the end of the show, in the grand finale, he took a bunch of flowers, that seemed to have grown out of his hat, and presented them to Tasha. She took them with a big smile, then kissed the frog Brett had won for her and gave it to the clown.

Brett stared. Now he knew who the frog had reminded her of. He gave her an amazed, questioning look but Tasha was watching the ring and waving as the performers, the clowns bringing up the rear, filed out of sight. 'Another friend?' he asked as they stood up and followed the slow-moving audience from the big top.

'Sort of, I suppose.' She was holding the flowers and bent to smell them. They were yellow roses, he saw, and they were real. Giving him a speculative glance, she said, 'Would you like to meet him?'

He hesitated, finding himself deeply averse to meeting an ex-boyfriend, an ex-lover, someone who had been to bed with her, who knew her body intimately and who would have that knowledge in his eyes, in his voice. How could he shake the hand of a man who had touched her where he had not? So he said, 'Who is he?'

'A clown.' She paused, then added, 'Someone I love very much.'

For a terrible moment his heart lurched sickeningly, but then common sense reasserted itself as he realised that she had no reason to be so cruel to him, to taunt him. So there must be some other reason for her bringing him here. Was it another of the tests she set him, the traps he had to be constantly wary of? Keeping his voice even, he said, 'OK, let's go and find him.'

They didn't have to search; Tasha knew the way. When they at last got out of the big top she led him through the fairground stalls to an area where all the caravans belonging to the circus folk were parked, and straight up to an old-fashioned caravan that was all gleaming paintwork and polished chrome. She rapped on the door and almost immediately, as if he had been waiting for her knock, it was opened by a tall, thin, elderly man who opened his arms wide to her. Tasha ran up the steps to him and was enveloped in a tight hug.

After a couple of minutes, when the man finally

loosened his hold a little, Tasha turned and smiled down at Brett. 'Come and meet my grandfather,' she invited.

They stayed for nearly three hours. It was the early hours of the morning before they said goodbye, and even then the old man was reluctant to let Tasha go. 'You'll come again soon,' he insisted.

'Yes, Grandpop. Very soon.'

He walked with them to the car and in an aside to Brett said, 'Take care of her for me. She can be head-strong, you know.'

Brett smiled. 'I'm learning, sir.' He shook hands without any hesitation.

When they were in the car and driving back to London, Brett said, 'Tell me about him. Has he always been a clown?'

'No, he was a very respectable accountant until he was over fifty. But the circus fascinated him. He used to do a clown act to amuse me when I was a child, and that led to being an entertainer at children's parties in his spare time. Then, when my grandmother died, he took early retirement and joined the circus. He's been there for over ten years now and absolutely loves it.'

'But he misses you.'

Tasha nodded. 'Yes, but we see each other as often as we can.'

'He's your mother's father?'

'Yes.'

'What about your parents?'

'My mother died in an accident when I was quite young. My father was working abroad at the time and stayed on there. In time he remarried.'

'So your grandparents brought you up.'

'Yes.' Tasha grinned. 'I had the most wonderful childhood. I was thoroughly spoilt.'

'No wonder you're so close.' Reaching out, Brett took hold of a lock of her hair that nestled against her neck and curled it round his finger. 'Thanks.'

'For what?'

'For letting me learn more about you.' She didn't say anything so he said, 'Have you any more surprises in store?'

She gave him an amused glance. 'Of course.'

'I hope they're all as nice as your grandfather.'

She liked that; it pleased her. 'Tell me about your family,' she invited.

He shrugged. 'My parents are both retired and are golf fanatics. I have two sisters, both married and with children.'

'Do you see them much?'

'Not as much as I should, probably. I left home at eighteen to go to college and never went back. My parents moved to a smaller house and it was their home, not mine; it held no memories for me. They have their lives and I have mine. We meet up for family occasions, and sometimes for Christmas, but that's it really.'

'It sounds lonely.'

'I didn't mean it to.' He shrugged again. 'That's the way it is. We're just not that close. But they see my sisters and their families quite often.'

Tasha gave him a disturbed look. 'You must miss out on a lot.'

'Not really. It would be different if I was married and had kids, then I'd make sure they saw their grandparents, met their aunts and cousins, but we get along OK. If they need me they know they only have to call.'

'But it means that you've been looking after yourself for a long time.'

'Yes.'

'Perhaps that's why you're like you are,' she said musingly, half to herself.

'What am I like?' he asked, immensely interested to know her opinion of him, how she thought of him.

She didn't answer for several minutes and Brett thought that she was going to ignore the question, but it seemed that she had been pondering her reply because she eventually said, 'Enigmatic is, I think, the most appropriate word I can find. Behind the sexual side of your nature, I feel that you have hidden depths, things you don't want to share. Perhaps can't share.'

Brett was stunned by her perceptiveness; he'd always imagined he'd managed to fool her. Afraid that she might probe further, he quickly said, 'I'm very willing to share the sexual side. Any time.'

'Oh, Brett!' She made a face at him. 'Stop being a conventional male.'

That made him laugh. 'I'll try. I'll try!'

But the dangerous moment had been averted and he talked of other things until she dropped him off at his house, almost casually telling him that she would be busy for some time.

'Does that mean we can't see each other?'

'I really must concentrate on my programme. My boss has started asking when he can schedule the filming.'

Alone, Brett realised that he was walking on ever

more treacherous ground. What if Tasha wanted to meet his family? The fact that he'd been a journalist for more than ten years was bound to be mentioned. And he knew with utmost certainty that if Tasha ever found out he would lose her. But not, perhaps, if they were already lovers. He *had* to get her down to Cornwall and make her his, make her need him so much that she wouldn't care about his past.

He let a few days go by then bought a large seashell and sent it to her with a note. 'Hold this to your ear and you'll know the sound I wake to every morning at my cottage.' Over the next couple of weeks he sent her various books, both fiction and non-fiction, all set in or glorifying the county of Cornwall, and these were followed by a photograph of the cottage, an old building of weathered grey stone set in a garden ablaze with foxgloves. Brett daily expected some reaction, but it wasn't until the day he had a hot Cornish pasty delivered to her office that Tasha at last phoned him.

'I think you're trying to tell me something.'

'Could be.'

'I'm very busy, Brett.'

'How's it going?'

'Very well. I've interviewed nearly everyone I want to see and I just have to work out how I want the programme to go before we start shooting.'

'Have you got a lap-top?'

'I can borrow one. Why?'

'You could take all your notes down to Cornwall and work on your script there in peace and quiet. No phone calls, no interruptions,' he added persuasively.

'No one wanting to make love all day long?'

'Only all night long,' he assured her, but not meaning it.

Tasha laughed and he heard her speak to someone, then she came on the line again and said, 'That was my boss. He wanted to know if you were the nut who sent the pasty. And he says if you're into sending things from Cornwall he'd liked some clotted cream.'

'Tell him you'll send him some yourself when you're down there. When am I going to see you?'

'Why don't you stop by the office and take me out for a drink tonight?' Tasha invited.

They arranged to meet at six, but Brett got held up in the rush hour traffic and then had difficulty parking so was a little late. Tasha was standing outside the building, chatting to a man who had just come out. There was something vaguely familiar about him, so Brett paused in a shop doorway and let the man leave before he joined Tasha. She was wearing a deep green fitted jacket and a Black Watch tartan skirt that was well above her knees. She looked sensational and he felt a thrill of pride to be with her. He wanted to feel the joy of possessiveness and ownership too, but that emotion was still denied him. But he kissed her lingeringly before saying, 'Who was that? A colleague?'

'My boss.'

'Oh? What's his name?'

'Joe Hedley.'

Brett cursed inwardly, immediately recognising the name. Hedley had once worked on a news programme for a national broadcasting network and they had sometimes covered the same stories. If Tasha mentioned Brett's name Joe Hedley would be bound to remember him.

'Have you told him about me?'

Tasha looked a little surprised. 'No. My private life is just that—strictly private. He wouldn't have known about you at all if you hadn't sent the pasty. It was very good, by the way; I had it for lunch. Who did you get to make it for you?'

'What makes you think I didn't make it myself?'

'You mean you can cook on top of everything else?'

'Of what else?'

'Oh—just being gorgeous and handsome and sexy, I suppose.'

He stopped and caught her round the waist, stared down at her in delighted disbelief. 'You paid me a compliment!'

'Well, don't get carried away; I don't intend to do it too often in case you get big-headed.'

'I don't think I stand in much danger of that.' Keeping his arm round her waist, he began to walk on, then said, 'I didn't make the pasty.'

'I didn't think you did,' Tasha laughed. 'Who did?'

'I got my next door neighbour to do it.'

'What's she like?'

'In her late twenties, blonde and very curvaceous,' he responded at once.

Tasha gave him an old-fashioned look, not sure whether or not to believe him. 'Is that supposed to make me jealous?'

'Are you?'

'No.'

Brett sighed theatrically. 'She also happens to adore her husband and is very pregnant with her third child.

And her mother lives nearby and supervised the
pasty.'

'You see how right I was not to be jealous,' Tasha
said with satisfaction.

'I feel very frustrated,' Brett complained. 'It's all
very well getting to know me as a person but when
am I going to become a sex object?'

That made her gurgle with laughter, the sound rich
and happy. 'Believe me, you wouldn't like it.'

'How do I know when I haven't tried it? I'll let
you exploit me any time.'

She threw him a quick glance, surprised at his
choice of the word, but he gave her a mock-lascivious
look and she laughed again. They found a pub and sat
outside on the pavement under a big sunshade. It was
a very warm evening and there were many workers
there, having a drink before they caught the train
home, avoiding the worst of the rush hour. Like Brett,
most of the men had taken off their jackets and re-
moved their ties. Tasha, too, took off her jacket and
draped it on the back of her chair. The sun caught her
hair, turning it into a gleaming, burnished halo around
her head, and her long lashes cast misty shadows on
her cheeks. Brett thought that she had never looked
lovelier, but then he seemed to think that every time
he saw her.

Glancing at him, Tasha saw the flame of desire in
his eyes, in the sharpened features of his face. Often,
when she caught him looking at her like that, she
would raise a mocking eyebrow and turn away, but
tonight she looked him fully in the face and slowly
ran the tip of her tongue across her lips. It was so
sexy that Brett could have laid her on the pavement

and taken her there and then! He let out his breath in a deep sigh of frustration, and said feelingly, 'Jezebel!'

Demurely, she said, 'But, Brett, I'm awfully thirsty.'

He got up to get the drinks and Tasha watched him go, enjoying his back view in the tight jeans. There must have been a stack of people waiting to be served because Brett was gone for some time. After a few minutes a middle-aged man carrying a briefcase walked by, stopped, then came back and sat down on the seat next to her. 'Hello. You look rather lonely. My name's Rob. What's yours?'

'I'm with someone,' Tasha returned calmly.

'Obviously no one of any importance if he can only afford to bring you to a place like this. How about having dinner with me? We can go anywhere you like. The Savoy, The Trocadero, just name it.'

'Thanks, but I'm not interested.' And Tasha turned her head away.

But the man only moved closer along the bench and put a familiar hand on her shoulder. Angrily Tasha shook him off and swung round to tell him to get lost, but before she could do so she heard Brett behind her say, 'Take your hand off her, you creep.'

The man's head came up and he paled when he saw the venomous look in Brett's face as he loomed over him. Quickly he got to his feet and picked up his case, but as he moved away he said spitefully, 'What else did she expect when she makes eyes at every man walking by?'

Brett had put down one of the drinks he was carrying, but at this he lunged forward and grabbed the man by his belt, then, holding his terrified eyes, he very deliberately tipped the pint of beer he was carrying down the front of the man's trousers. 'Explain that to your wife, you old goat.'

The man scuttled away and some girls sitting at a nearby table gave Brett a cheer as he came to sit with Tasha again. He grinned at them and said with satisfaction, 'That should suitably dampen his ardour.'

But Tasha gave him a tight look. 'Did you have to react so strongly? In fact, did you have to react at all?'

Brett gazed at her in complete astonishment. 'You did want to get rid of him, didn't you?'

'I'm quite capable of dealing with types like him myself. I didn't need any help, and I certainly didn't need the big he-man act.'

'Did you really expect me to just stand by and let that creep paw you?'

Tasha's eyes grew cold. 'You paw me—you do it all the time.'

'That's different,' Brett protested.

'Is it? And do you suggest I use that method to dampen *your* ardour the next time you get the hots for me?'

Becoming annoyed now, Brett said shortly, 'You're being ridiculous.'

'Am I? Am I really?' Bright spots of anger came into Tasha's cheeks. Standing up, she said curtly, 'Thanks for the drink, Brett. Why don't you go and get yourself another one? You might even get to drink it this time. And sit with those girls, why don't you? They obviously admire your ''me Tarzan, you Jane'' act.' She gave him a fulminating look. *'But I don't!'* And, turning on her heel, she strode away.

Brett caught her up in three strides, furious at her lack of understanding, furious that she could do this to him. Catching her arm, he swung her round to face him. 'What the hell's the matter with you? Anyone would think you *wanted* the man to pick you up.'

'How dare you say that?' Tasha returned with equal anger.

'So what is this about?'

'It's about taking over, about you thinking you have the right to interfere whether you're needed or not.'

'Any other woman would be grateful for—'

'I am not any other woman,' Tasha interrupted acidly. 'I'm *me*. And if you haven't realised that yet then we might just as well say goodbye now, because—'

Brett shook her. 'I told you never to say that to me again. How can you build up something so trivial into—?'

'It wasn't trivial. Not to me.'

Struggling to contain his anger, Brett ran a hand through his hair, then said, 'So what are you trying to say?'

'Just don't interfere in my life.'

His voice became urgent. 'But I want to be a part of your life; you know that.'

'Be part of it, yes—but don't try and take it over. OK?'

It wasn't, and he still thought she was making far too much of the incident, but he wasn't yet sure enough of her to openly argue, so he held up his hands placatingly and said, 'OK. I'm sorry. It won't happen again. Now, will you come back and have that drink?'

Tasha hesitated, aware that his apology had been too pat, too makeshift for him to have really thought about her feelings. But maybe he would later; she hoped he would. So she nodded. 'Yes, all right.'

Brett got himself another drink, inwardly cursing; he had fully intended to exert all his powers of persuasion tonight to get her to come to Cornwall with him. His hopes had been high but now they were at zero. He guessed she would at least make him wait for a couple of weeks just to punish him, and fully expected her to be cold to him for the rest of the evening. But he was prejudging Tasha on his experience of other women.

She wasn't like other women, as she'd told him, and he was gratified to find that she smiled at him when he went back to her and behaved as if the nasty little incident had never happened and that nothing had come between them. They had their drinks and he told her a couple of anecdotes that made her delicious laugh turn heads, and she looked at him with that special look, the one that made him feel he was the only man in the world. Really, he supposed, he couldn't blame that old creep for trying to chat her up, but to say that his feelings for her were the same was utterly ridiculous.

He was even more pleased when she took him back to her place and cooked him a meal, which they ate by candlelight, sitting at the window and feeling the air gradually cool with the night. Afterwards he stretched out on the settee and she came to lie beside him, her head on his shoulder as they listened to a new classical CD. But it wasn't long before he tilted her head and took her lips. As always, she immediately set his blood on fire. Soon his kisses became demanding, impassioned, and his fingers, fumbling in his eagerness, pulled off her top and undid the delicate lace of her bra.

He groaned as he touched her, his breath already hot and unsteady. He had never known such a deep ache of need, such *hunger* for a woman. It was so strong it was like a physical pain that sawed at his insides. He took her nipple in his mouth and it was so wonderful that he wanted to eat her. He wanted to kiss every inch of her, to leave no part of her that he hadn't caressed and fondled, that he hadn't loved.

His hand moved down to her legs. They were bare, soft like silk, long and beautiful. He caressed her ankle, moved to her knee and up to her thigh. There was sweat on his face and his breath was burning in his rasping throat. His hand tightened on her thigh and he kissed her fiercely, then said her name in raw, desperate need. 'Tasha! *Oh, God, Tasha, I want you.* I can't go on like this. Not any longer. I'm mad for you. Crazy.'

Her own voice unsteady, she said breathlessly, 'Brett, I—'

But he wouldn't let her finish. 'Do you know what you're doing to me? Do you?' Catching her hand, he put it on himself and held it there. 'Here. Feel for yourself. You can't leave me like this, my darling, you just can't be so cruel.'

Slipping her hand from under his, she raised it to his face, made him look at her. Her eyes in the semi-

darkness were like brilliant jewels, but she frowned
and said, 'Do you really think I'm being cruel?'

He groaned, then said, 'We've known each other
for two months. If you don't know me well enough
to trust yourself to me by now...' Forgetting his own
deception, he said harshly, 'What more is there to
know, for God's sake?'

Rolling off the settee, Tasha got to her feet and
looked at him. Her hair was dishevelled and a lock of
it hung down over her shoulder to caress her breast,
to touch the nipple that he had made hard with
aroused desire. To stop himself from pulling her down
to him and taking her Brett had to ball his hands into
fists so tight that they shook with frustration.

As if reading his thoughts, Tasha gave a small
smile and said, 'All right.' For a moment he thought
that she meant that they could make love now, this
minute, and he could hardly breathe with ecstatic
delight, but then she added, 'I'll go to Cornwall with
you.'

'And then...?'

She nodded, and a mischievous look came into her
eyes as she reached down and ran her fingertip over
the stretched, rising material of his jeans. 'And then
we'll see what we can do about this.'

'When?'

'This weekend.'

'Friday?'

She laughed. 'OK, Friday.'

'It's a long time till Friday.'

'Two whole days,' she mocked.

'You're a witch, Tasha. A gypsy witch.'

He had to be content with her promise, and he went

home at least with something definite to look forward to. First thing in the morning he rang the neighbour who looked after the cottage for him and asked her to get it ready for Friday evening. 'Get lots of food in,' he instructed, adding by way of excuse, 'Just in case the weather changes,' even though the forecast predicted that the glorious summer weather would go on indefinitely.

It was impossible to concentrate on work so Brett didn't try, he just savoured the anticipation, the excitement of knowing that she would soon be his. On Friday he turned up at her flat much too early, and in a large comfortable car that he'd hired for a month. Because he had every intention, once he got Tasha down there, of keeping her with him at the cottage as long as he possibly could.

She came out to meet him carrying a suitcase and another bag slung over her shoulder. Tasha's eyebrows rose when she saw the car. 'What's this?'

'It will get us there quicker,' he explained.

Laughing, she came up to him and sent his senses reeling as she leaned close and moved against him. 'I'm all for that.'

If he hadn't known her will-power he would have thought her as randy as he, but maybe, now that she was committed, she felt free to let her feelings take over. He certainly hoped so. Because he just knew that once Tasha freely gave herself then there would be no woman more passionate, more sensual.

They put her case in the boot and she slung her bag on the back seat. In minutes they were on their way, threading through the traffic and heading for the motorway that would get them to the cottage in just a few hours. Brett had to put the thought out of his mind and concentrate, but every now and again he would look at her and be unable to resist reaching out to put his hand on her knee. Then she would smile at him, her eyes promising him the most wonderful night of his life, and, supremely happy, he would drive on, wishing the miles away.

He'd made sure that he had enough petrol for the whole journey so didn't have to stop, but, two thirds of the way there, the mobile in Tasha's bag began to ring. She knelt on the seat to get it, then said, 'Hello? Sarah? What is it, what's the matter?' She listened, tried to speak, but whoever was calling just kept talking. Brett couldn't hear the words but he realised that the voice was female and seemed to be highly excited. Then Tasha said, 'Sarah, listen to me. It's OK. I'll come. Yes, as soon as I can. No, you mustn't talk like that. Please don't even think about that. I've said I'll come. I won't let you be alone. Yes, soon. Bye.' She flipped the phone closed and looked across at Brett.

'No!' he said forcefully.

'Brett, I have to go back. It's Sarah. Clyde has walked out on her and she's dreadfully—'

'I don't care!' he said violently. 'I'm taking you to Cornwall. You're not going back!'

CHAPTER FIVE

'BUT you don't understand. Sarah sounds suicidal! I've just got to—'

'That's rubbish! She must have a hundred people she could have called. Why you?'

'Because I'm her closest friend. Because her family are away on holiday in America.' Tasha's voice rose forcefully. 'Because it's me she wants, damn it!'

Made bitter by angry disappointment, Brett bit out scathingly, 'Yeah? And she just happens to need you now, this minute. How very convenient.'

Tasha stared at him. 'And just what is that supposed to mean?'

He threw her a furious glare. 'Maybe you fixed it for her to phone. Maybe this is just a trick you've pulled to stop us going to bed together. Just another damn delaying tactic.'

'How dare you accuse me of such a cheap ploy?' Her face taut with anger, Tasha said, 'Will you please pull off at the next exit?'

'No. We're going to Cornwall.'

She flipped open her phone. 'If you don't, I'll call the police. Tell them you're abducting me.'

He laughed in harsh disbelief—but then looked at her face. He remembered her independent spirit, then cursed, 'Damn it all to hell! You would, too.'

'There would be no point in saying it if I didn't mean it.'

His mind full of the greatest disappointment and humiliation he had ever known, Brett tried pleading. 'Surely there's someone else, Tasha. You know how much this means to me.'

'I know how much it meant to us both—not that you've given my feelings a thought.'

'Then how could you possibly even contemplate—?'

'She's a friend, Brett. She needs me.'

'And don't I need you? Need you far more than Sarah ever could?'

'No. No, you don't. You're not in trouble, and she is. My friends are very important to me, Brett. They always will be.'

In a voice full of anguished defeat, he said, 'She's using you.'

'That's what friends are for.' Tasha paused, then said more gently, 'I am what I am, Brett. You can't change me.'

He didn't believe that, but didn't say so. He was sure that if they'd only managed to reach his cottage and become lovers then he would have been able to mould her as he wished. And she would never have agreed to leave him for some friend's so-called emergency. The sign for a service station came up and he turned into the slip road, determined to try to make her change her mind. When he pulled up in the car park, he turned to her and took hold of her hand, said as persuasively as he knew how, 'Look, let's talk this through.'

'Whenever men say that it just means they intend to talk you into doing what they want,' Tasha said in a flat statement. 'It won't work, Brett. I'm sorry, but I'm going back to London.'

Furious that she wouldn't even give him a chance, he said curtly, 'Oh? How?'

Withdrawing her hand, she was silent for a moment, then said tightly, 'I suppose that means you won't take me?'

'Why the hell should I?'

With dignity Tasha said, 'I could think of a great many reasons, but maybe you aren't the kind of person who would know about—'

'Don't tell me what kind of person I am,' Brett cut in. 'You promised to come with me tonight and now you've broken that promise just because some friend has made a panic call. Damn it, you didn't even try to argue, to explain. You just came straight out and said you'd go back, and to hell with me.'

'Ah,' Tasha said mockingly. 'Is the spoilt little boy not going to get the toy he's been promised?'

His jaw jerked out and he stared at her. 'That was a very cheap remark.'

'And just what would you call the way you're behaving?' Not waiting for his answer, Tasha opened the door and got out of the car.

Brett immediately came after her. 'Where do you think you're going?'

'You know very well where; back to London.'

'And what about me?'

'Me! I! Mine!' She spat the words at him. 'That's all you can say, isn't it? All you think about is yourself. *Your* disappointment, *your* frustration. Your lonely bed tonight. But what about Sarah's lonely bed? She's been living with Clyde for two years, but he's just walked out because she asked him to make a commitment to her. This is the worst moment of her life, but you want me to ignore her, to turn my back on her.' Her voice grew jeering. 'And all because you just can't wait to satisfy your sexual cravings.'

Brett's jaw thrust forward and his hands balled into fists. 'This is much more than just sex and you know it.'

'No, as a matter of fact I don't know it.' Tasha faced up to him, her eyes flashing lightning and her face taut with anger. 'And nor, I think, do you. You're blinded by your own libido. You'll say anything to get what you want because you're a typical male, completely selfish when it comes to your own desires, and—'

Not waiting to hear any more, Brett strode back to the car, pulled out Tasha's suitcase and threw it on the ground. Then he slammed down the boot, got into the car and, without looking at her, drove away. He had never known such fury in his entire life. He slammed his fist against the steering wheel in his anger, hit it again and again. How dared she call him selfish? How dared she? Serve her damn well right that he'd abandoned her. Let her get back to London to her friend who was more important to her than he was. If she could. She'd certainly never be able to hire a car at this time of night, he thought with some satisfaction. Not that Tasha was the kind of girl who would let something like that stop her. Brett suddenly had a vision of her thumbing a lift, from a lorry driver probably. His heart went cold. She was a woman alone and anything could happen to her. Images of

rape and murder filled his mind. And it would be his
fault; he'd as good as kicked her out.

His anger completely gone, Brett felt sweat on his
lip as he looked for signs of an exit from the motorway, a junction where he could turn round and go
back for her. He was filled with a great dread, a fear
for her that consumed every other feeling. It was
miles before the next turn-off, and then he had to
drive all the way back to the service station, but it
was on the opposite side of the motorway. He ran
across the bridge which connected the two, at one
minute filled with panic, the next confident that he
would find Tasha where he had left her, sitting on her
case, waiting for him to return for her. She wasn't in
the car park. He ran into the building, searching the
restaurant, the shop, the snack-bar. Then it occurred
to him that of course Tasha had crossed the bridge
herself; she would have had to if she was going back
to London. So he ran back and started searching all
over again. But she was gone. There was no sign of
her.

Feeling sick with desperation, he ran back to the
car, found his phone and called her mobile number.
After a moment she answered, and the relief was so
overwhelming it took his breath away and he couldn't
speak.

Her tone cold, Tasha said, 'If that's you, Brett, then
you'll be pleased to know I'm on my way to London.'

'Are you all right?' His voice was ragged.

'I'm surprised you bother to ask.'

'Damn it, Tasha, are you all right?'

There was a pause, then she said, 'I'm with a very
nice family in their people carrier. Parents, grandpar-

ents, two children and a dog. The dog is on my lap. Goodbye, Brett.'

'Wait, I—'

But the phone went dead.

Going back to his car, Brett sat in it for a long time. The memory of his disappointment came back but was as nothing now to the fear he had felt for her. And the worst of it was that deep down he knew Tasha had been right; he had been completely selfish. His thoughts and emotions had centred entirely on himself. If he had been reasonable about it they wouldn't have quarrelled. OK, the trip to Cornwall would have been postponed, but at least it would still have been on the cards. As it was...

He couldn't envisage their ever getting together again. He had lost her. Lost the wild, free spirit he had come to admire so much. Now he would never be able to make her his. Never be able to possess that beautiful body. His heart filled with desolation and he began to feel angry with her again. But his thoughts came to an abrupt stop as he realised that he was once more thinking only of himself. His mouth twisted wryly. But what man didn't think that way? It was a natural, inbred instinct to want a woman as an extension of himself. He wanted Tasha as *his* lover, *his* mistress, in his bed. He wanted to possess her in every way and to mean everything to her. He wanted her to make herself *his*.

There seemed no point in going on to his cottage now, but then there didn't seem to be much point in going back to London either. He'd made arrangements to be away for an indefinite period and he felt too sick at heart just to go tamely back and try to take up his life again. Besides, he needed time to think. Putting the car in gear, he once again headed west.

It was dark when he reached the cottage, the headlights cutting a swathe through the night as he went slowly down the narrow, tree-hung lane that led down to the sea and the cove in which the cottage stood in lonely isolation. He didn't bother to take his case from the car at first, instead letting himself in and going over the house in ever-growing chagrin. It all looked so perfect for romance: a fire laid in the big hearth, just waiting to be lit and for them to make love on the deep rug in front of it, the bed made up and the curtains drawn. But the wild passion he had imagined so often wouldn't now take place within its enveloping covers or on the soft, old-fashioned counterpane. Opening a window to lean out, he could hear the sound of the waves breaking on the shore, but there was no moon and he couldn't see them. They wouldn't now bathe in the sea, or stroll on the beach, or find some deserted piece of sand sheltered by rocks where they would make love.

Brett tried to think of Tasha, tried to be reasonable and detached, but it was well nigh impossible when he was alone here in his bedroom. She should be back in London now, knocking on her friend's door, offering comfort and commiseration. He could almost imagine them running men down, Tasha explaining that she, too, had been let down tonight. That hurt, because he had at least come to his senses and gone back for her—but she wouldn't know that, of course. Even if he managed to reach her long enough for him to tell her, she probably wouldn't believe him. Banging the window shut, he ran out of the house and down to the beach, where he pulled off all his clothes and then ran into the sea, swimming out strongly against the waves until he was tired, then floating on his back to rest before, his frustration eased by physical effort, he turned and swam strongly back to the shore.

There he dragged on his jeans but carried the rest of his clothes, dumped them indoors and went back to the car for his bag. It was only then that he noticed the bag that Tasha had left on the back seat. Inside it was a lap-top computer and a bulging documents case.

In London, Tasha spent the whole night and the next day listening to Sarah, not attempting to offer advice, which she knew would be a waste of time, but just being there for her. Sarah was in tears most of the time and a nervous wreck whenever the phone rang in case it might be Clyde wanting to apologise, to say that he was coming back. Then, when he'd been gone for forty-eight hours without a word, Sarah started to get angry. That lasted for about another day, but then she broke down into tears again because it was the anniversary of their moving in together.

It was an exhausting time for Tasha and she had little leisure to think of work. It wasn't until several days later that she realised she'd left all her stuff in Brett's car. She cursed inwardly, hoping he'd noticed it was there and not just returned the hire car. Sarah had now reached the suffering in silence stage, her mouth set into a martyred line. But at least she was over the worst and had agreed to go and stay with her parents, who were due home from their holiday the next day.

Anxious about her work, Tasha picked up the phone and called Brett's house in Docklands. All she got was his voice on the answering machine; she left no message. Later she tried a couple more times, but when he still didn't answer she came to the conclusion that he must still be down in Cornwall. She went to call him there but remembered he'd said he never switched his phone on to receive calls there, willing to put up with the inconvenience for the sake of peace and solitude. The next afternoon she drove Sarah to her parents' house. They were embarrassingly profuse with their thanks for her kindness to their daughter, and insisted she stay to dinner. They even wanted her to stay the night, but Tasha made an excuse and managed to get away. She had only gone a short distance before she pulled into a lay-by, sat in thought for a couple of minutes, then took out her road map book and looked up the quickest route to Cornwall.

It was a long drive, and towards the end she had to stop often to consult the map, but the full moon was almost as bright as day and at last she found the right lane and drove down to the cove. Parking the car behind the house, she was relieved to see that the hire car was still there. But the back seat was empty. There was a light on downstairs, but when she knocked there was no reply. The door was unlocked. Pushing it open, Tasha called Brett's name. Again there was no response. She went round the place, liking everything she saw, but there was no sign of Brett. Maybe he had walked to the nearest village to the pub or something. She decided to go down to the beach to wait for him. Slipping off her shoes, she walked across the soft sand dunes, then paused. Brett was sitting on the beach just above the tide line. He was hunched forward, his chin on his knees, and seemed to be deep in thought.

Tasha stopped to watch him, thinking that there was a dejected set to his shoulders. Presently he got up and she expected him to come back to the house, but instead he took off his clothes until he stood naked. He looked very beautiful in the moonlight; it silvered his skin until he looked like a shining marble statue. A god for people to worship. A perfect sculpture of perfect manhood. Without glancing round, he walked into the sea and began to swim.

Slowly Tasha walked down to the water's edge. She felt profoundly moved by what she had seen. The naturalness of his actions, his silhouette in the moonlight, his arrant masculinity, had stirred her deeply. Somehow it belittled their differences, made modern-day competitiveness between the sexes seem of no importance. So must primitive man have stood when it was his God-given right and duty to provide for and protect his woman. That was what his superior strength and power had been intended for. The supreme being on earth.

Tasha felt a sudden and terribly deep yearning for such a simple life, for the basic clearness of that existence. Lifting her hands, she undid the clips that held back her hair and let it fall, then shook her head from side to side to send it swirling around her head, as if throwing off the yoke of the twentieth century. Without haste she took off her clothes, one by one, and dropped them on the sand beside Brett's. When she, too, was naked, she tilted her head towards the starlit sky and laughed aloud, a silvery note lost in the sound of the waves. Then she ran into the sea.

Brett was floating on his back and thought first of all that it was a strand of floating seaweed that had brushed against him as he felt a feather-light touch running down his leg. But he grew rigid with shock as the sensation became more definite and he realised it was fingertips that were stroking him. He gasped, jerked over onto his front, a vision of a floating dead body large in his mind. But then he heard a low laugh that he recognised and he was consumed by incredulous, unbelievable happiness.

'Tasha!'

She laughed again and dived away from the hand he reached out to her, came up behind him and blew in his ear. Brett gave a shout of laughter and turned to try to catch her. But she swam away, turned and splashed him, the water a phosphorescent arch in the moonlight. He joined in her game as she got tantalisingly close but then flashed away from him, chasing her and deliberately letting her get away, although he could have caught her several times. Once he grabbed her arm and pulled her near enough to kiss her and run his hand over her. He found that she was naked, and it so blew his mind that he slackened his hold and she slipped away from him again. This time she dived a long way and he couldn't find her. He called her name a few times and looked wildly round, then saw her wading out of the sea.

He swam towards the shore, felt sand under his feet and stood up. Tasha was standing where the beach shelved, small waves breaking around her feet. Naked and supremely lovely. Waiting for him. Brett gave a hoarse cry of mingled joy and surprise, of excitement and wonder. Taking a step towards her, he held out a hand and said hoarsely, 'Are you real—or are you a mermaid come to torment me?'

She smiled. Reaching out, she took his hand and carried it to her cheek, held it there for a moment, then slowly guided his hand down her length. Over her breast, down her slim waist to the flat plane of her stomach, and on down to her thighs. 'Now do you know whether I'm real or not?' she whispered.

The hand that she still held against her was shaking and Brett's breath was a rasping gasp in his throat. His body was like a volcano about to erupt, his blood on fire, his flesh trembling, his mind almost unable to cope with the frenzied heat of desire and anticipation. Suddenly he could stand it no longer. With a groan of real pain he dragged her to him and began to rain kisses on her mouth, her eyes, her throat. He made small, muttering sounds of agonised need and held her tightly against him, wanting her too desperately for gentleness.

She moved her hips against his and he cried out with the agony of delight it gave him. He stumbled and they fell onto the sand, the water licking at their bodies. Tasha put her arms around him and hungrily claimed his mouth, returning his kiss with wild passion, with all her heart and soul. They rolled on the sand, first one of them in the water and then the other as they wrapped their legs around each other, kissing frantically, each moaning out their cries of frustrated sensuality.

Brett heaved himself over her and spread her legs. He looked down at her for a moment, at her hair like a silken halo around her head, at her face sharpened by desire and her mouth and eyes eager for love. Then he came down on her, thrusting with all his strength, so that she cried out. But her voice was drowned under his own great shout of triumph, under his groans of gathering delight and the shuddering tremors of his body as he climaxed. He did so very quickly, completely unable to control himself, but when he would have moved away Tasha wouldn't let him go. Instead she wrapped her arms and legs round him and moved with him, her breath hot and gasping, her lips kissing his throat and his mouth, her teeth nipping his ear, his nipples, sending shock waves of wild delight coursing through him, so that within minutes he found himself again making love to her, his need for her as frantic as it had been the first time.

Rolling on top of him, Tasha held him tightly within her and showed him no mercy, carrying him along, using him to fuel her own mounting excitement until he thought that he could no longer stand such prolonged and frenzied pleasure, that his heart would burst and he would die of ecstasy. But then Tasha cried out in a long breath of agonised wonder and set him free at last to erupt in voluptuous abandonment all over again.

For a while they lay, temporarily exhausted, in each other's arms. Then Brett pushed wet strands of hair from her face and kissed her deeply. 'That was wonderful,' he said hoarsely. 'So wonderful!' He chuckled. 'I felt like a volcano erupting.'

Tasha smiled and reached down to stroke him. 'I like your Vesuvius.'

'If you go on doing that he will probably erupt all over again.'

'Such threats,' she mocked, and scooping up a handful of water she let it trickle over his chest, then bent to lick his skin. 'You taste of salt and the ocean, of trade winds and arctic snow. Of little streams that grow into great rivers and water that carries the sound of whales and the call of seagulls.'

Brett was enchanted. Sitting up, he pulled her onto his lap and began to wash the sand from her breasts, letting the water run down over her still delightfully hard nipples, then following the trail it made with his fingertips. 'What made you come back?'

'Sarah's parents came back from their holiday to-day, and I drove her down to stay with them.'

'Has she recovered?' Despite his happiness there was a dry note in his voice.

'No,' Tasha replied evenly. 'I think it will take a very long time for her to do that, and I doubt if she will ever forget.'

But Brett wasn't interested in her friend's problems. The waves were washing partly over them, sometimes covering Tasha's loveliness as they swirled and frothed over her legs, then drawing back so that she was revealed to him again, almost as if the sea were playing a tantalising game with him. Reaching out, he began to stroke her gently. He felt her stiffen, then she looked at him—and smiled.

Suddenly frantically hungry for her all over again, Brett lifted her in his arms and came to his feet in one lithe movement. Forgetting their clothes, forgetting everything else, he almost ran with her back to the house. Her arms about his neck, Tasha started to nuzzle him, to kiss the length of his jaw, bite his earlobe. He groaned, stumbled, paused to take her mouth and kiss her with fierce passion. He groaned again as he dragged his mouth from hers and went on to the house, kicking open the door and heading for the stairs and the bedroom.

They didn't get that far. The stairs were low and narrow so that there was no way he could carry her up them. Setting her down, Brett reached to take her hand and lead her upstairs, but Tasha leaned against the wall and pulled him close. Putting her hands low on his waist she held him there while she moved against him, setting his loins on fire, the while kissing him avidly.

. He was already aroused, and such additional sensuality was both an overwhelming delight and an exquisite torture. 'Oh, God,' he groaned. 'I'm not sure I can take this.'

'You'll live,' she breathed unsteadily. 'Believe me, you'll live.'

She pulled him yet closer, held him as he took her, using her body to lift him to dizzying heights of sexual pleasure that he had never known. And later, when they finally reached his bedroom, she was again utterly wild and abandoned, as he had always dreamed she would be. Once she gave herself Tasha had absolutely no inhibitions. It was the most primitive, wonderful night he had ever known, leaving him utterly exhausted but feeling that he had the strength of a lion, that he could easily conquer the world. That the world, in fact, was already his. He finally fell asleep in sublime happiness and slept deeply and dreamlessly far into the morning.

At first, when he slowly came to, Brett thought that he had been having the most fantastic dream, but then the strange languor of his own body brought memory flooding back. At once fully awake, he reached out for Tasha, but found the bed empty. In a sudden panic, he leapt out of bed and ran to the window, then gave a great sigh of relief; her car was still there. He looked round for his towelling robe but couldn't find it, so ran downstairs as he was.

Tasha was in the kitchen and was wearing his robe. She looked absolutely fantastic in it, her hair fastened back off her face with one of his ties, and her face bare of make-up. He thought that she had never looked so beautiful. Without hesitation he crossed the room and took her in his arms, then kissed her long and lingeringly.

With a jug of orange juice in one hand and a glass in the other Tasha was able to put up little resistance, not that she tried. When Brett lifted his head at last she laughed up at him. 'Well, good morning.' Then she quite frankly let her eyes run over him.

'Sorry,' he grinned. 'But someone stole my robe.'

'Oh, that's OK. I'm all for gratuitous nudity—so long at it's male, of course.'

'You could always give my robe back,' he pointed out hopefully.

'Not until you go down to the beach and collect my clothes. They're all I've got.'

Brett's eyebrows rose. 'You didn't bring a suit-case?'

'No. Coming here was a sort of spur-of-the-moment thing.'

He frowned, the ego-comforting idea that she'd

been just waiting for her friend to be out of the way before she came rushing back to him suddenly dissolving. 'You didn't plan to come down?'

Seeing his frown, Tasha set the things down and put her arms round his neck. 'Not last night. The idea was to go home from Sarah's parents and come down this morning, plus suitcase. But then I suddenly thought, why wait? So I came straight here.'

It wasn't strictly true, but it immediately dissolved his frown and made him laugh. 'Only you could do that. What do I get if I go and get your clothes?'

'Arrested, I should think, if you go like that.'

'Who's to see?'

'I saw two boats full of sightseers go by the cove this morning. Are you the sight they've come to see?'

Brett grimaced. 'They're the only drawback in the summer.' Undoing the belt of the robe, he slid his hands inside. Her skin was warm, like finest silk, so firm and yet so pliant beneath his hands. 'You're so lovely,' he murmured, kissing her neck. 'So very lovely.' He stroked her length, making himself randy. 'Come back to bed.'

Tasha laughingly pushed him away. 'Later. Go and get your trousers on, King, then get my clothes before they're washed away by the sea. You wouldn't like me to be left without a thing to wear, now, would you?'

'Do you really want me to answer a silly question like that?'

'All right, how's this? No clothes, no sex. Get it?'

'I'm on my way.' He turned and strode for the door.

'Hey!'

He glanced down. 'Oh, yeah.' Reaching out, he plucked the robe from her shoulders, then just had to kiss her indignant face before he shrugged it on.

When he came back, carrying their clothes, Tasha was no longer in the kitchen. He yelled out to her and she called back from the bedroom. He found her sitting up in the bed, wearing one of his shirts and drinking a glass of orange juice. She looked completely relaxed and at home, almost as if she was meant to be there. As far as Brett was concerned that was exactly where he wanted her. 'Your clothes, ma'am.' He dumped them all on a chair, took off the robe and got into bed with her. 'Who said you could borrow that shirt?'

'Do you object?'

'I think you should return it at once.'

She put her tongue out at him, then laughed when he immediately leaned forward and kissed it.

'You've got the cutest tongue.'

'Want some orange juice?'

'Please.'

She poured some for him and he leaned back against the pillows in utter contentment; he couldn't remember when he had felt so good, so happy and so fulfilled. Letting his fingers run down her spine, he said in smug triumph, 'I always knew you'd be a wildcat in bed.'

She glanced at him over her shoulder, her mouth pouting, her eyes wanton. 'You thought about it, huh?'

Just that look turned him on. His voice dry, Brett said, 'I've been able to think of little else but what it would be like since the day I met you.'

'And now you know,' she said softly.

'And now I know what an incredible woman you are,' he agreed. 'Last night was—just fantastic, my darling.' He waited, but when she didn't say anything said in a mock-patient voice, 'You are now supposed to say that you did at least enjoy it.'

An imp of mischief came into her blue eyes. 'Oh, really? Was I supposed to enjoy it, then?'

'Minx! Why don't you finish that and come here?'

She took a sip from her glass, her eyes on him, then ran the tip of her tongue over her lips.

'God, I love it when you do that. It's so damn sexy. Drink it up.'

'I'm in no hurry.'

'Tasha!'

She laughed at him. 'Is Vesuvius on the boil again?'

'Definitely.'

'Well, in that case…' She put the glass aside and moved over to him. 'This time I'll remember I'm supposed to enjoy it.'

He was left in no doubt that she did, her moans of pleasure filling his ears, her tremors of delight thrilling his body. And afterwards, when they were both spent, he held her close, thinking that this had been the best time yet, that he could never have enough of her.

Brett would have liked to stay in bed all day, but Tasha slipped to the bathroom to shower and when she came out began to dress. 'I shall have to go out and buy some clothes,' she informed him. 'Which way is the nearest town?'

'Why bother? I shall only take them off again,' he said complacently.

'If I don't buy some, then I'll have to go all the way back to London to pack a case.'

He was immediately out of bed. 'I'll be with you in two minutes.'

'You don't have to come. I can manage.'

'Are you crazy? Now that I've finally got you here I'm not going to let you out of my sight.'

'But your book? I wouldn't want to stop your work.'

'To hell with the book! Don't move.'

He showered and shaved swiftly, pulled on clean jeans and shirt, then went to find her. Tasha was standing among the foxgloves in the garden and he caught his breath, so fierce was the wish that he could paint. She made such a vibrant picture, with her red hair blowing about her head, the carpet of colour reaching above her waist and the cloudless blue of the sky behind her. But he could do the next best thing. Backing into the cottage, Brett found his camera and stood in the doorway to take a photograph that he knew couldn't be anything but perfect. Tasha was unaware of him; she was looking away from the house, her head tilted a little towards the sun and the sea, a small smile of contentment on her lips. It was a smile that matched his own wide grin, that spoke of a perfect night of sexual fulfilment.

Impatient to see the finished result, Brett took the film from the camera, then strolled outside. 'Ready to go?'

'I'll just get my bag.'

Brett drove into the nearest town, the car roof open,

and they joined in the throng of tourists strolling the streets. Their only disagreement came when Tasha had chosen some clothes and he went to pay. But she immediately took out her own credit card and handed it to the assistant. 'I'll buy my own things.'

'But I want to get them for you.'

'Thanks, but no.'

Aware of the assistant's curiosity, Brett waited until she was out of earshot before putting a possessive hand on Tasha's waist and saying, 'Surely now I'm allowed to buy things for you, darling?'

She gave him a direct look. 'No. I haven't given you that right.'

Brett's eyes widened in surprise and then his face tightened. 'Doesn't giving me your body mean anything, then?'

'It means a great deal.' Tasha's eyes softened and she put up a hand to stroke his face. 'I think you know that. But it doesn't mean that I belong to you. I'm a person, independent of what we do together, and you must let me stay that way.'

He was disappointed but tried not to show it; he wanted her to be dependent on him, entirely dependent, but obviously that one night, erotic as it had been, hadn't been enough. But there was time yet. He would make her so sated by sex, so fulfilled by it, that soon she wouldn't be able to live without it. Bending to kiss her, he murmured, 'OK, we'll do it your way.' But he didn't mean it, and in that moment he decided to make her fall in love with him.

CHAPTER SIX

THEY had lunch in the town, then bought enough supplies to last them for a few days before heading back to the cottage. Already Brett wanted her again. Walking through the town with Tasha, a negligent hand on her shoulder or waist, to let everyone know that they were intimate, had been a pleasure out of all proportion to what he had known in the past. He had walked with other women before, women he had taken to his bed, but he had never felt such pride before, such triumph in possession. Perhaps it was because Tasha had played hard to get for so long, until his desire for her had become all-consuming. Or perhaps it was because he'd thought he'd lost her and then she had come to him of her own accord. Or, there again, it could be simply because it had been such extraordinarily great sex.

When they got back to the cottage, Brett took in the food while Tasha carried the shopping bags full of her new clothes. She went to take them upstairs but found that Brett had just dumped the groceries and was behind her, chasing her. In the bedroom he didn't even give her time to take her clothes off, his eagerness for her was on fire and had to be satisfied now, now!

It was only afterwards that he undressed her slowly, unbuttoning her shirt to stroke and caress her breasts, pulling down the zip of her skirt and running his hand inside. Tasha stood it for a while, then reached out and began to take off his clothes, too. When they were naked they made love again, but slowly, oh, so slowly, each endeavouring to give the other maximum pleasure, to lift them to new heights of sensual excitement. Brett felt that his body had become an instrument on which Tasha could play the most delectable tunes, first taking him close to rapture then away again, to give him a small respite, before stroking and kissing him into brimming delight that threatened to consume him until she drew back and his quivering body began to relax again.

'You witch!' he groaned. 'You enchantress.' Opening his eyes a little, he saw her bending over him, her eyes heavy with desire. 'Come here,' he said thickly, and pulled her down to kiss her. Then he began to do some teasing of his own.

It was quite some time afterwards before they found the strength to move. Tasha went to the bathroom and when she came back, still naked, began to sort through the things she'd bought that afternoon. 'Can I use one of the drawers in the chest to put my things in?'

'Sure. Just sling my stuff into one of the others.'

Brett watched her, glad that she hadn't dressed or wrapped a towel round herself. He wanted her to feel that it was natural to be naked with him, to be always ready for more lovemaking. Her body was pale, showing that she hadn't sunbathed much that summer, but there was a faint flush of colour on her arms and face from their walk round the town that day. He decided he wanted her to be tanned all over, with no white bikini marks. Tomorrow he would take her down to the beach, find a private spot, and they would both sunbathe naked—and make love as often as he could manage it.

Having taken his clothes and put them into another drawer, Tasha went to replace them with her own, then paused. Reaching into the drawer, she drew something out and looked at it for a long moment. It was an earring, a rather garish one of rolled gold with a large red-coloured stone dangling from it. Clipping it onto her own ear, she pushed back her hair, then finished putting her clothes away before going to join Brett on the bed.

He reached for her happily and would have kissed her, but she turned her head so that her profile with the earring was towards him. Even then he hardly noticed, nuzzling her neck, until she swung her head and the earring hit him. Blithely unconcerned, he saw it at last and said, 'Just one earring?'

'Only one had been left behind in the drawer.'

'In the…?'

'Do you bring all your women here, Brett?'

Unable to read anything in her face, he brazened it out. 'My sisters bring their families here for holidays, you know. One of them—'

'Liar!' She pinched him hard.

'Ouch!' Brett hoped it meant she was jealous. If she was, then she must care about him. He held up his hands in mock-surrender. 'OK, I don't know who left it behind.'

'So you have brought other women here?'

He shrugged. 'I'm no monk, Tasha. You must have realised that by now.' He put his hand on her thigh. 'Just as you aren't exactly inexperienced.'

'So we're to play tit-for-tat?'

'You started this,' Brett pointed out.

'A typically masculine remark.' Swinging her legs off the bed, Tasha began to dress.

'Hey, what are you doing? I thought we were going to spend the afternoon in bed.'

'I don't feel like it.' Tasha pulled on a blouse and knotted it round her waist. 'Where have you put the work I left in the car?'

Brett sat up and folded his arms, a grim look to his mouth. 'Is this supposed to be some kind of punishment, Tasha?'

She glanced at him and raised her eyebrows. 'For you abandoning me at the service station, do you mean?'

'I went back for you.'

'Really?' The word wasn't openly disbelieving, but neither was it pleased. 'Where's my work, Brett?'

Capitulating, knowing that in this fight he would never win, he said, 'Downstairs. In the cupboard by the fireplace.'

She went to go out through the door, but stopped and took off the earring, then tossed it to him. 'Here. You may want to return this.'

Catching it, Brett threw it with unnecessary force into the wastepaper basket. But Tasha had already gone. Moodily he got out of bed to dress, thinking that he had lost control of the situation, which wasn't something he was used to—not where women were concerned at least.

When he went downstairs Tasha was seated at a gateleg table, which she had opened, and had set up the lap-top, her papers piled beside it. Getting himself a beer, he leaned against the wall nearby. She looked up at him and smiled. The smile surprised him; he'd expected her to be sulky if not downright cold. Brett hesitated, then his jaw set; he didn't want to start this particular conversation but he knew it had to be done. Abruptly, he said, 'I read through your notes.'

Tasha became very still. 'You had no right to do that.'

'I knew that.'

'So—why?'

'Because, from the little you'd told me, I'd begun to suspect that the programme you were planning could be dangerous.'

She turned to look at him, her eyes frowning. 'Dangerous?'

'For you—and for the women you've been interviewing.'

'How could it possibly be—?'

'Think about it, Tasha,' he interrupted forcefully. 'These are famous men you're dealing with, not nonentities. Famous people have power, otherwise they wouldn't be able to exploit the women in the first place. If just one of them finds out what you're planning—and you can be sure as hell it will be found out—then they'll use every means in their power to stop you. And powerful men play dirty, Tasha. The more powerful the more unscrupulous and ruthless they can be. Just talking to these women will have shown you that.'

'I'm not afraid.'

She lifted her chin as she said it, a fierce light of determination in her eyes. She looked so incredibly beautiful that he felt something like pain in his chest, but Brett ignored it as he said with all his persuasive power, 'You're just a young woman at the outset of your career. Some of those men could break you in an hour, make sure you never work in television again. They could even have you hurt physically. An ''accident'' in your car, being mugged in the street. Even a fire in your flat,' he added with deliberate brutality. She gave an incredulous gasp, but he went on, 'You've picked on men in high places and they've a lot to lose. Do you really think they'd take a chance on you exposing them when they could put you out of the way?'

Tight-lipped, she said, 'Yes, you're right; it's because they are in responsible positions that I chose them, and that's why they should be exposed for what they are. Are you saying that I should drop the whole idea?' Tasha added indignantly. 'That I should let them get away with it?'

'You're digging up too much dirt. It will only rebound on you. At the very least untold pressure will be put on your boss to stop the programme. Has he read your notes? Does he know exactly what you intend?' She didn't answer, looked away. 'I thought not. I bet you're deliberately keeping him in the dark, stringing him along. When he finds out, the programme will never be shown. But there are other ways to—'

But she interrupted angrily, 'I won't give it up. Those women are putting their trust in me to avenge them.'

He looked at her, saw that she was completely unconvinced, so he said deliberately, 'Are you avenging them—or yourself?'

She stiffened. 'What do you mean?'

'You told me about the college tutor who tried to rape you. You plan to denounce him in this programme, don't you?'

'So what if I do?'

Striding over, Brett put both hands on the table and leaned towards her. His voice harsh, he said, 'So take a look at your motives for doing this programme. You may have convinced yourself you're on a crusade for others, but in reality you're completely governed by your own desire for revenge. The only reason you went looking for those women was to pad out the programme. You want to get your own back, Tasha, and you're using those women to help you do it. You are *exploiting them,* just as ruthlessly as the men who used them.'

Tasha's face had gone pale, but there were bright spots of anger in her cheeks as she said, 'That isn't true.'

'No? Have you thought about what will happen to those women once the programme is shown? You only have their word for it that they've been used. Have you tried to corroborate their stories?'

'How can I when there weren't any witnesses? The very basis of sexual exploitation is that it's between two people and is done in secret.'

'Exactly! So what's to stop every one of those men suing you? They'll take you to the cleaners, Tasha. You'll still be paying off your debts when you're a hundred years old.'

'I'm not afraid of that.'

She had such courage that his heart smote him, but he said, 'It's not just you. Those women will be sued for slander, too. Have you told them that could happen, warned them of what they might have to face? No, of course you haven't—because all you can think about is getting revenge on the man who hurt you. *You,* Tasha. This is what it's all about.'

In sudden rage, she pushed herself to her feet and burst out, 'Why shouldn't I have justice? I got thrown out of college. I lost my chance of a degree. And I had done nothing. *Nothing!* But he wasn't even punished. It was all hushed up. He was just pensioned off. They even made a ceremony out of it and the college gave him a presentation! It was a clock. They gave him a damn clock as a reward for raping his students!'

Suddenly tears were coursing down her cheeks. Brett caught her to him and held her close in his arms. 'Oh, my sweet. My poor darling. I know it's unfair. Life *is* bloody unfair. But you can't do this. Believe me, my darling, you've got to let it go.'

She sobbed against his shoulder, murmured incoherently. Brett stroked her hair, said soothing words of comfort and kissed her forehead. 'I know it's rotten, but you'll hurt yourself far more than you'll hurt him. Believe me, sweetheart.'

Her tears still flowed and she made a protesting noise, but not so vehemently as before. But it was a while before she gulped and raised her head from his shoulder. Brett gave her his handkerchief and Tasha wiped her face, then gave a croaky laugh. 'I can't believe I broke down like that. I've never cried about this before. Not even when it happened.'

'Maybe that's been the problem; you've been bottling the whole thing up all these years, letting it grow out of all proportion.'

She looked at him, her eyes still wet and deeply troubled. 'Could those women I've interviewed really be harmed if I go ahead?'

'I think you already know the answer to that one,' he said gently.

She sighed in deep unhappiness. 'Why are men so cruel to women?'

Realising that she had given in, Brett smiled and said lightly, 'Who knows? In another generation it might well be the other way round.'

But Tasha shook her head. 'Somehow I don't think so.'

'Hey, this isn't like you. Where's your optimism?'

She gave him a sombre look. 'I'm sorry I soaked your shoulder; I'm not usually this weak. This stupid. This *feminine*. This—'

Brett stopped her words with his mouth, kissing her gently. 'You just got lost for a while, that's all. But you're OK now, aren't you?' There was a question in his voice; he wanted to be sure that she'd been persuaded.

Stepping away from him, she said, 'I promised those women. Especially that girl who works as an air stewardess. She's depending on me.'

'She won't thank you if something happens to her because of it. She's in a foreign country working for an all-powerful man. She wouldn't stand a chance, Tasha.'

Her eyes widened, then she said bitterly, 'You seem to know all about man's inhumanity to woman.' Then she shook her head a little and sighed. 'Sorry, I didn't

mean to be nasty. I think I'll go for a walk, try and
sort things out in my mind.'

'Do you want me to come with you?'

'No.' She shook her head. 'I'd rather be alone. I've
got a lot of thinking to do.'

Tasha walked down to the beach. The tide was out
and she kicked off her shoes and began to walk along
the water line. The sun was low in the sky, deep red,
turning the shore and the rocks to a delicate pink and
leaving shadows where her feet sank in the wet sand.
She realised that since she had first had the idea for
this programme she hadn't even considered the consequences it might have. It had seemed such a beautiful way of getting revenge at last. And the same for
all those other women. She had been looking for a
way of getting her own back for such a long time,
and she could still remember the thrill of excitement
she'd felt when she'd first realised she could do so
through this programme.

It had all seemed so simple and straightforward. A
friend had told her about someone she knew, a personal secretary to a powerful businessman, who'd had
it made clear to her that she was expected to be available sexually whenever they went abroad or to con-
ferences together. Career girls talked to each other,
confided their problems, their secrets, and one had led
her on to another, until Tasha had known she had the
makings of a really good, controversial programme.

Looking back, Tasha now saw that once the idea
of taking part in it herself had taken root in her mind,
then all qualms had been lost beneath the obsessive
idea; she was going to get her own back at last. But
Brett had ruthlessly made her question her own mo-

tives. She didn't thank him for it. She *wanted* revenge. Needed it badly. And she would have been quite happy to take any consequences arising out of her actions. But what about the other women she'd planned to use? Use. Her thoughts dwelt on the word. Brett had said she was exploiting them herself, that they would be doubly injured if she went ahead. But maybe some of them, too, would be happy so long as the men who'd used them were exposed for what they were. Perhaps she could ask them, perhaps the programme could still go ahead. But did she have the right to let them risk it?

Tasha kicked moodily at a sea-shell. She knew she was just kidding herself; there was no way now that she could go on with the programme. All that work, all the hopes and all the trust that had been placed in her would all be for nothing, would all go to waste. And, once she told her boss that she'd decided to abandon the project, it would probably cost her the job with the television company as well.

She felt stunned by the suddenness of realising how completely selfish she'd been, but most of all by the way she had blinded herself to the consequences. It made her feel dreadfully unsure of herself, not only in this but in every aspect of her life. There seemed to be only one thing of which she was absolutely positive, and that was that right now she needed Brett very badly. She needed his strength and his closeness, his clear-headedness and—most of all—his comfort. With a little sob, Tasha turned and ran back to the cottage.

He was waiting for her at the door. Catching her in his arms, Brett held her for a long moment, saying nothing, just letting her feel his strength enfolding her. Then he picked her up and carried her into the sitting-room. He had lit the fire, and he laid her on the deep, soft rug in front of it.

They stayed at the cottage for three more days—days of unbridled passion. But their relationship had subtly changed. It was no longer an equal partnership; Brett was now the more dominant one. Tasha, made vulnerable by guilt and uncertainty, had turned to him for comfort and let him take control, and without realising it was becoming dependent on him. Her work was abandoned, rejected, and she even went to destroy her notes, to throw them on the fire. But Brett stopped her. 'No, don't do that. Never throw work away. Here, give them to me; I'll put them away for you.'

He locked them in his desk, then took her down to the beach again to swim and make love. For him those days were near perfect; he gloried in her willing body, in the feminine weakness that had made her so submissive. Soon, he thought, she would admit that she was in love with him. But, strangely, it wasn't somehow as satisfying as he had expected. He was vaguely aware that there seemed to be something missing, but he couldn't figure out what. But then, he was so sated by sex that he hardly had the energy to think about anything else.

It was Tasha's mobile phone ringing that broke up the idyll. It was her boss demanding to know where the hell she was and what was happening about the programme. Reluctantly, feeling full of guilt, Tasha told him she'd be in the office the next day.

Listening to the call, Brett came up behind her. Put-

ting his arms round her waist, he kissed her neck, then
said, 'You don't have to go back.'

Tasha leaned her head back against his shoulder
and put her arms over his. 'But I must.'

'Do you want to?'

'No.'

'Why not?'

Part of the truth was that she didn't want to have
to go back to face the consequences of her own actions, to face reality. She didn't want to have to contact all those women she had interviewed and tell
them that the project had been ditched. To do so was
to acknowledge failure, to admit that she'd made a
terrible mistake, one that could have led to complete
disaster if it hadn't been for Brett. Tasha had come to
see that now and to be grateful, so she told him the
other part of the truth, which was what he wanted to
hear. 'Because I don't want this to end, of course.'

'Sweetheart.' Unbuttoning her dress, he slipped his
hands inside. She was naked underneath; he had soon
put a stop to her wearing a bra. He caressed her gently
at first, then more firmly, expert now at what aroused
her the most. 'We still have the rest of today and all
tonight,' he said thickly. 'We must make it special.'

'How?'

'I'll think of something.' He turned her within his
arms so that he could bend to kiss her breasts.

She watched him through half-closed lids, giving
little gasps as his mouth pulled at her so-sensitive nipples, and she smiled a little, thinking that they must
surely have explored every way to have sex during
the last few days. Sitting down on a chair, Brett pulled

her astride him so that he could go on kissing her while they made love.

That evening they cooked a spectacular meal which they ate by candlelight by the open windows, the sound of the sea soft in the background. They drank a lot of champagne, and later went hand-in-hand down to the beach where they undressed each other and waded out through the waves, the phosphorescent spray licking their legs, their thighs, their chests. In the water they kissed, touched, caressed, until they were both aroused to fever-pitch.

They had made love in the sea before, but this time Brett picked her up and carried her back across the beach to the garden behind the cottage. There he laid her down among the thick bed of foxgloves, their riotous colours lost in the moonlight. But the scent of them filled the air as her body crushed the tender blooms. Tasha gave a small sound of protest, but Brett caught hold of some of the flowers and scattered the petals on her, letting them fall from his fingers onto the soft, shadowed curves of her body.

They felt like butterflies' wings on her skin, and where Brett's fingers had bruised them the perfume was so strong, heady as any wine, filling her senses. He took her with controlled passion, deliberately holding back to prolong her pleasure, making her cry out, moan with frustrated desire. His own breathing ragged, Brett lifted himself on his elbow and gripped her waist with his free hand. 'Look at me,' he commanded. 'Open your eyes. Look at me.'

Tasha did so with difficulty, it was almost impossible when he was making her gasp like this, when he was giving her so much pleasure.

'Do you want to go back, Tasha?'

'N-no. I told you so.'

'Do you care about me, then? Do you?' He rasped out the words, his voice rough with the effort it was taking to control himself.

'You know I do. You're…special.' He drew back a little and she put her hands on his shoulders, feeling suddenly empty and desperate, yearning for him again.

His hand tightened convulsively on her waist. 'Then say it.'

Her eyes opened wider and she frowned. Brett was poised above her, his face all black and silver planes and angles in the moonlight. She could see the intensity in his eyes and guessed what he wanted. But she said, 'Brett?' on a questioning note.

'Say it,' he commanded again, his voice harsh with insistence.

She hesitated, feeling coerced, but suddenly felt unsure of herself all over again. And right at that moment he was everything to her; she wanted his closeness, didn't want it ever to end, so she said breathlessly, 'I—I love you. I—yes, I know I love you.'

'My darling!' His voice filled with happiness. He stooped to kiss her, and now he released his own pent up passion, thrusting forward to lift them both to the heights of prolonged excitement.

Afterwards, he murmured happy words of endearment, kissed her and paid her lavish compliments. Once Tasha would have rejected such flattery, but now she found she liked it; it made her feel pleased that her body, at least, wasn't a failure, that it could give such evident pleasure. And she was glad that Brett seemed to want her to love him so badly. It made her feel needed and gave her back some of her confidence, even though at the back of her mind she sensed that by saying she loved him she was also giving away a great deal of her independence.

Eventually they went back into the house and to bed, and early the next morning were standing together in the shower when Brett said, 'I want you to move in with me.'

Tasha looked up, startled. 'You mean here?'

'I mean that I want you with me wherever I am. Either here or in London.'

'Oh, sir, this is so sudden!' she prevaricated, putting on a mock coy simper.

'No, it isn't. You want to be with me, don't you?'

'Well, yes, but—'

He put his finger over her lips, then kissed her. 'No buts. As soon as you get to London I want you to give up your flat and move your stuff into my place. I'll give you a key so that you can start moving in straight away.'

'Aren't you going to London?'

'No, I have to go away for a week or so, to do some research on my book.'

Tasha had thought that he'd already done as much research as he needed, but didn't question it. He had done hardly any work during the last few days, having devoted himself entirely to her, and she felt guilty about that. But she said, 'Brett, I don't know. I'm not used to living with anyone, and—'

'If you love me, as you said, then you'll want to live with me.' Picking up the soap, he began to lather

her back. 'Besides, I've an idea I'll go insane with lust unless I have this gorgeous body of yours in my bed every night. Now that I know how wonderful making love to you can be, I don't ever want to stop.'

'So I've noticed,' Tasha laughed. 'Hey, you don't have to give me a demonstration... Brett, I have to get back to London...Brett!'

Later, when they were dressed, he gave her a key to his house. 'I'll expect to find you waiting for me there when I get back.'

'I don't know how long it will take to get my place sorted out.' Tasha sighed. 'And I'll have to put in a lot of time at the office—that's if I still have a job after what's happened.'

'Don't worry,' Brett told her as she packed. 'You're too good to get the sack. Just point out that the company would have been sued into bankruptcy if you'd gone ahead. Sell your boss another idea, tell him you've been working on it.'

'I wish you were coming with me.' For Tasha to say such a thing was unlike her, and was convincing proof of her growing dependence on him, of the fact that she had become so insecure.

'I wish I could. But I have to do that research for my book. I'll be back in London as soon as I can.'

He kissed her goodbye and waited at the door until the little yellow car was out of sight, then Brett went into the sitting-room and opened the drawer where he had locked away Tasha's notes. Taking them out, he selected those that referred to her interview with the air stewardess and put them into his briefcase, then ran upstairs to pack a case and within half an hour was heading for the nearest airport.

Tasha got into a row with her boss, but accepted his anger so meekly that he was completely thrown and merely told her to come up with something else—fast! Going back to her flat, Tasha went through her files looking for inspiration but found that she was strangely unsure of herself. Where formerly she would have been fired up with enthusiasm for a project, now she felt reluctant and doubtful. Taking out the videos of the previous programmes she'd made, she watched them again, looking at them with new eyes, wondering if she'd exploited people to make those, too. What if she made another mistake? She wished Brett was there so she could discuss it with him, but he would be deep in the research for his book. Feeling deeply depressed, she rang Sarah, who was equally low.

'I take it you haven't got back with Clyde?'

'No, and I don't want to now. I'm going to sell this place and find myself somewhere new to live. Where have you been? I rang you several times while I was staying with my parents.'

'I went down to Cornwall for a few days.'

'Tell you what; why don't we doll ourselves up and go and find ourselves a couple of men?' Sarah suggested.

'I don't need a man. But I would like to talk. How about dinner?'

They met late at a Soho bistro and began to discuss Sarah's decision to sell her flat. 'I've decided it's best to make a clean break,' she told Tasha. 'To completely cut Clyde out of my life and start over. I've thrown out everything he left behind, burnt his photographs, donated all the presents he gave me to Oxfam. There's nothing left of him in my life now.'

'Except memories. They aren't so easy to lose.'

'No—but I'm trying.' Sarah looked up. 'How about you? How are you getting along with the writer? What was his name?'

'Brett King. OK. It was his place I went to in Cornwall. He has a cottage by the sea.'

'You stayed with him? You must be getting serious about him, then?'

A troubled look came into Tasha's eyes. 'He's special, yes. And he's great in bed. But…I don't know. He wants me to move in with him and I suppose I agreed. I care about him. I really do care, but…' Her voice trailed off.

'You don't sound very certain. Usually you're so sure of your own feelings.'

'Yes, I suppose so. But something happened down in Cornwall. I was working on a programme about sexual exploitation, was perfectly happy about it, but Brett made me see that what I was doing was all wrong. It's shaken me. I seem to have lost all my confidence.' She told Sarah about some of the women she'd interviewed, of the air stewardess that she felt really bad about.

'It sounds as if he was right. You could have been playing with fire. But if you're going to move in with him you must be really keen on him. Are you in love with him?'

Slowly, exploring her feelings, Tasha said, 'I feel that I want to be with him, especially since this happened. I'm worried in case I choose a project that's going to work out badly again. I feel I need his advice.'

'But that's work. How do you feel about him as a man?' Sarah persisted.

Tasha shook her head. 'I told him I loved him. He seemed to want me to so much. And I owe him a lot. But I just don't know. Telling someone you love them is really committing yourself.'

'Don't I know it. Clyde was always wanting me to tell him I loved him, but look what he did to me!'

They talked on, finding some comfort in sharing their problems, and both went home to their lonely beds.

Finally making up her mind, Tasha began to work on a new project and started looking round for someone to take over her flat and to pack some of her things. But she didn't do so with any great urgency. Brett had rung her several times and had said he wouldn't be home for at least another couple of weeks.

Towards the end of this period, when Tasha was at the office one morning, Sarah rang her. 'Have you seen today's *New Millennium?*' she asked, naming a national newspaper.

'No. Why?'

'You remember what you were telling me about the stewardess who was being sexually exploited by a Middle Eastern potentate? Well, there's an article in this morning's paper that sounds exactly like the situation. Tell you what, I'll fax you a copy.'

Tasha waited by the fax machine and eagerly tore off the sheet, then stood spellbound as she started to read. There could be no doubt that it was about the

same girl. Although it didn't give Anne's name, all
the facts were the same, and there was a photo of the
bedroom on the plane. The *New Millennium* was a
quality newspaper and it had treated the subject in a
serious way, but the article was a scathing accusation
against the magnate. It pointed out that he was supposed to be a philanthropist, and was involved with
many charities, and yet he had no compunction in
exploiting a woman who was dependent on him for a
livelihood. Once she'd read it through, Tasha's eyes
ran over the article, eagerly looking for the reporter's
name, but it just said, 'By our Middle Eastern corre-
spondent'.

Tasha had contacted the stewardess to tell her she
wouldn't be going ahead with the programme as soon
as she got back from Cornwall, so it looked as if the
woman had gone to another reporter with her story.
Tasha hoped fervently that Anne—and the reporter—
knew what they were doing. She went through the
article again, more slowly, and stopped, puzzled. She
recognised a phrase in the text, not as something she'd
been told, but as an observation she herself had written when she'd been interviewing the girl. But that
was impossible. Unless... Tasha became very still, her
mind racing. Only one other person could have seen
what she'd written and that was Brett. And he had
stopped her from destroying her notes, had them all
locked away down in Cornwall.

Sitting down at her desk, Tasha gazed into space
for a while, then checked her watch and put a call
through to Hong Kong. When she got through she
said, 'Guy, how are you? It seems ages since your
farewell party.' They talked a little and then she said,

'Your friend Brett King—you remember he was at the party? I'm looking for a reporter for a programme I'm doing, and I seem to remember he said he was a journalist. Do I have that right?' She listened, then said, 'Oh, I see. He used to be a journalist. Which paper? The *New Millennium*. Thanks, Guy, I expect I'll be able to contact him there. When are you coming over?'

Her face was very tense, very cold when she put down the receiver. Tasha then flipped through her file of contacts and found the name of a girl she knew who worked for the newspaper and called her. She talked very persuasively for a few minutes and the girl promised to call her back. Gripping her fists, Tasha waited. At last the call came. 'You're right,' the girl told her. 'The name of the reporter who wrote the piece was definitely Brett King.'

CHAPTER SEVEN

IT WAS another week before Brett returned to London. In that time he rang Tasha several times but she didn't take the calls, merely listening to the messages on the answering machines. Brett's voice came over as warm, intimate, full of confidence in his possession of her. He spoke of when they would be together again, how he couldn't wait to take her to bed. His tone was rich with sexual need and also the sure knowledge that she shared it, that it would soon be satisfied. The later messages asked whether she had moved into his house yet, said that as she hadn't answered the calls to her flat he hoped to find her waiting for him there. But there was still no uncertainty in his voice; he was still very sure of her.

Tasha listened to the last message along with Sarah, who was at the flat with her.

'What are you going to do about him?' Sarah asked when the answering machine clicked off. 'Ditch him?'

'Oh, definitely.' Tasha was coldly decisive. 'But he used me, and I don't intend to just let him get away with it.'

'That might be difficult. He sounds clever.'

'Oh, he is. But he thinks that he's brainwashed me into letting him take control. Which is where he's wrong,' Tasha added venomously.

'Will you tell him you've found out he wrote the article?'

'That he plagiarised my notes, you mean? You can bet your life that if I do he'll try and talk me round, use sex to dominate me.' She got angrily to her feet and paced the room. 'The rat! He deliberately set out to undermine my confidence, to make me think that I was making a huge mistake in putting together the programme. And like an absolute fool I believed him. I've never felt so unsure of myself in my life. And all the time he was just using me—!' Breaking off, she glared at Sarah. 'I've got to think up something that will absolutely devastate him.'

'You could take him to court for plagiarism,' Sarah offered.

With a dismissive gesture, Tasha said, 'No, that wouldn't do any good. It would cost the earth and take too long. Don't forget, he still has all my notes; he only has to destroy them and then it would be my word against his. And anyway, to sue him just isn't personal enough. It has to be something that will not only knock him for six but will get rid of him at the same time.'

'Can't you just tell him that you've met someone else who's far better in bed?'

'That's an idea!' For a moment Tasha contemplated the thought with some pleasure, but then frowned. 'Somehow I don't think he'd believe me. There can be few men who are better lovers than Brett. The sex side of it was really good. Really good,' she repeated, remembering. 'That's why he'll use it to subdue me again.'

'Maybe he won't try,' Sarah suggested. 'He's a man, isn't he? Now he's got what he wants he'll probably drop you, instead of the other way round.'

But Tasha shook her head firmly. 'No. You heard his message on the phone; does that sound like he wants to be rid of me? No, my guess is he wants to use the rest of my notes, to do newspaper articles on all those other cases too. But even I, stupid fool that he thinks me, would be likely to notice if he did that. So he needs to talk me into letting him use them.'

'Yes, I see. So he'll try to hang onto you like grim death. It really would have to be something mind-boggling, then. Especially if you want to frighten the life out of him at the same time. What on earth could you do to...?' Sarah's voice faded as she looked at Tasha and saw that she had come to a stop, her eyes widening as an idea came to her. 'You've thought of something!'

'Yes. Yes, I rather think I have.' Tasha's face gleamed with excitement. 'I think I've come up with the very thing to put the fear of God into Brett and get rid of him at the same time.'

'On a personal level?'

Tasha smiled, her eyes full of vengeful triumph. 'Oh, yes, on a very personal level.'

'Tasha?' Brett's next call came while she was at the office a couple of days later, and this time she didn't duck it. 'Hey, what happened to you? I've been leaving messages for you everywhere.'

'Sorry, I've been away,' she lied glibly. 'Doing research for my new programme. The boss wants it in a hurry because I ditched the last one. I only got back late last night and fell into bed completely exhausted. How about you? How's your research going?'

'Fine. All done. I'm at home. I expected you to have moved in but none of your stuff is here.'

'Like I said; I've been working like a mad thing, shooting all over the place.'

'Well, let's get together tonight. Your place or mine?' Brett said with a suggestive chuckle, still totally sure of her.

Playing along, Tasha said, 'Anywhere,' on a breathy note.

He laughed. 'That's my girl. I've really missed you, darling.'

'And I've missed you,' she responded, her words warm but her face cold, adding for good measure, 'I can't wait to see you again.'

'I've got a great surprise for you.'

'Really? I've got lots to tell you, too. Where shall we meet?'

'How about you cooking a meal at your place?'

'OK. I'll see you there about eight, shall I?'

'Make it seven. I'll go crazy if I don't hold you in my arms again soon. I thought I was frustrated before we were together in Cornwall, but having made love to you, knowing how fantastic it was, I just long to be with you again every minute of the day.'

'Oh, do you really, Brett?' She made her voice full of gratified pleasure. 'You really have missed me, then?'

'Haven't I said so? You're mine, Tasha, now and for always.'

You mean until you get what you want out of me, you skunk! Tasha thought angrily as she replaced the receiver. Then smiled as she thought of the shock Brett was going to get tonight.

She set the stage carefully, going home early to shop and then prepare a meal. On the table she put a low flower arrangement with a stumpy candle in its centre. Even though it was still light outside, Tasha drew the curtains and lit only a couple of lamps. She plumped up the cushions on the settee and for good measure sprayed some of her French perfume in the air. Then she stood back and grinned with pleasure; the place looked like a film-set for a big seduction scene.

Brett arrived promptly, carrying a bouquet of flowers so large she could hardly see him behind it. Dropping it on the coffee-table, he swept her into his arms, lifting her off her feet, then laughed with sheer pleasure before kissing her deeply. It was a long time before he let her go, slowly lowering her until she was standing again but going on kissing her as if he never wanted to stop. Eventually, though, he raised his head and gave a long sigh of contentment. 'God, I needed that.' He smiled down at her, his eyes tender. 'You'll never know how much I've missed you.'

Tasha returned the smile, at the same time wondering how on earth she'd been so gullible. Was it his tough good looks or his air of worldly self-possession that had so seduced her? Or was it the wonderful way he made her feel when he kissed her? Even now, even though she knew him for the cheat he was, she had for a few minutes fallen under the spell of his kiss. His warmth and closeness got to her, making her remember how gloriously wonderful it had been when they made love. It took a huge effort to put those thoughts out of her mind, to feel instead the emotions that had been choking her since she'd found out the truth about him.

Inwardly she felt terribly angry and bitter. The anger was directed mostly at herself; she'd thought herself adult enough to judge character, but Brett had lied to her about his past almost from the first moment she'd met him, and she had believed every word he'd said. Well, then, let's see if she could be a good enough actress to deceive him in turn.

Playing with the hair at the back of his neck, she said huskily, 'Me, too. How are you? Are you OK?'

'Fine—except that I've scarcely stopped thinking about you every minute of the day. Here, these are for you.' Picking up the flowers, he gave them to her.

'Oh, how gorgeous!' Tasha buried her face in them so he couldn't see the malevolent look that came into her eyes. She had been right; such lavish flattery could only mean that he *did* want to use the rest of her notes.

They had dinner and Tasha was careful to keep the conversation light, impersonal. Brett, too, seemed to like it that way; he had every opportunity but he made no mention of the article that had appeared in the paper. He seemed on a high, laughing and smiling a lot, sometimes even smiling at his own thoughts. As well he might, if he thought that he was easily going to persuade her into letting him write a whole series based on her idea, her research, her contacts. Somehow Tasha managed to conceal her feelings. She cleared away after the meal and then Brett pulled her down to sit beside him on the settee.

'Don't you want to know what my surprise is?' he asked.

'Of course. But first...' Leaning forward, Tasha put

her hands on either side of his face and kissed him lingeringly. Then said breathily, 'It was so wonderful when we were together down at your cottage.'

'The best,' he agreed. 'The most fantastic time in my life.'

He sounded so sincere, the hypocrite! Mentally fuming, Tasha nevertheless made herself sound anxious and in need of reassurance as she said, 'You do care about me, don't you, darling?'

'You know I do.' His voice was thick. 'I want to share everything with you.'

But most of all my notes on the sexual exploitation programme, she thought vindictively. But somehow Tasha managed to smile and say, 'Why, that's marvellous. Because I have something I want to share with you.'

Putting his arm round her and looking deep into her eyes, Brett said intensely, 'I want us to be close, Tasha. Not just as lovers. I want us to be close in every way. As friends, companions, partners. To share everything. To work together, even. I just know we'd make a really good partnership. Together we can do anything, get anywhere we want to be.'

His voice, his eyes, were full of enthusiasm, and it was all Tasha could do not to show him up for the liar he was. But she pretended to be carried along with him, laughing with delight. 'Oh, yes! I'd love that too—especially now.'

'Now?'

'Because of my surprise that I have for you. It's really the most fantastic thing,' she said excitedly. 'At first I wasn't certain, but after what you've just said about sharing our lives I'm sure you're going to love it.'

He looked at her indulgently. 'And just what is this wonderful surprise?'

'I just know you're going to be absolutely over the moon.' She strung it out, enjoying herself, savouring the moment of revenge.

'What is it, then? Hey, come on, after all that build-up don't keep me in suspense.'

Smiling, watching his face, Tasha said, 'Why, it's simply that I'm pregnant, darling.'

CHAPTER EIGHT

TASHA watched as the smile became fixed on his face and the colour slowly drained from his cheeks.

'You—you're joking, of course.'

'Would I joke about something like that? Isn't it the most wonderful news?'

Taking his arm from round her shoulders, Brett sat back and looked at her. He blinked a couple of times, then said in a strangely odd voice, 'I thought that you had taken all the precautions necessary for this not to happen.'

'Did you? Obviously not.'

'Are you certain about this, Tasha?' His voice was stronger now, a little harsh at the flippancy of her answer.

'Quite certain.'

Brett could only stare at her, feeling completely devastated. All his senses seemed to have gone numb. He felt that he had stepped back in time, to an age when the Pill had never been invented. This was the kind of scenario that young men had nightmares about, but he had never thought of it happening to him; the women he knew were all too sophisticated and worldly wise to get caught in a trap like this. But maybe it was a trap that had been set for him. He looked searchingly into Tasha's face but could read no guilt there. She was watching him closely, studying his face to read his reactions, he supposed. He wasn't sure if he was behaving well or badly; it had been too much of a shock for him to start thinking straight yet.

Fumbling, he said, 'It must be early days yet. Isn't there a pill or something you could take to counteract it?'

'No, there's nothing I can take,' Tasha returned evenly.

Her eyes, so beautifully blue and clear, were still studying his face in an almost detached way.

Brett stood up, paced the floor a couple of times to try to start his brain functioning again, but the space was too confined. He felt like a prisoner in a padded cell and needed space and air. His tone abrupt, he said, 'I'm sorry, but you've given me a shock. I have to think about this. I'll be back.'

He strode out of the flat, yanking open the door and not bothering to shut it. Tasha could hear him running down the stairs, taking them two at a time as if all the devils of hell were after him, his steps fading until she heard the basement door slam closed behind him.

So it was over. Her ploy had worked far better even than she could have hoped. Going to the window, she saw that Brett was already passing under the street-light at the corner, then he turned it and was out of sight. That would be the last of him, then; she would definitely never see him again. And he would live in fear of her pursuing him for child maintenance for years. It was exactly what she had expected to happen; Brett had behaved like the liar and the cheat he was, running away at the first sign of trouble.

Tasha sat down on the window-seat knowing that she should be feeling good, that she should be pleased to be rid of him and that he would feel hunted for a long time to come. But somehow she felt only as if someone had slammed a door in her face, slammed it violently after having first led her through it to see and taste of the wonders on the other side. Lowering her head onto her hands, she wept.

Brett just kept walking, not noticing where he was going, but found that he had headed instinctively for the river. There were tourists strolling along, lovers holding hands, but he avoided them and leaned on the parapet, gazing unseeingly down at the lights reflected in the fast-flowing water. It occurred to him that he had gone to Tasha's flat today feeling better than he had done for years, certain that everything was going his way. He would tell her about the surprise he had for her, she would agree to the plan he had for the series on the sexual exploitation theme, and then they would go to bed together and make love.

He had thought about that so many times while he'd been away, his imagination heightened because he now knew every inch of her perfect body. In his mind he could hear her gasps of pleasure, even his own groans of overwhelming excitement. He had thrilled with anticipation as he thought about what he would do to her, how he would love her. But now... Sitting down on a bench, he put his head in his hands.

Never in his wildest dreams had he imagined this happening, especially not with Tasha. He began to think about what he knew or had heard about fatherhood: nights when you never got any sleep, smelly nappies, never being able to go out unless everything was planned weeks in advance. He remembered friends telling him bitterly of wives who suddenly lost interest in sex once they had a child, who were always too tired to make love. God, it sounded terrible! He saw his whole world changing, his freedom lost. He looked ahead, a bleak vision of the future coming into his mind. But then the vision changed a little and, slowly, his eyes widened and his gaze became transfixed. Brett let out a long sigh, turned, and began to stride quickly along the street.

Tasha had put on a CD but it had stopped playing long since. There were still only the lamps burning, but in a burst of rage she had flung open the window to get rid of the perfume that still hung in the air. Sarah had made her promise to call her, to let her know what had happened, but Tasha made no effort to do so. Her spirits were too low, too devastated for her to gloat with Sarah over the success of the trick she'd played. She was lying on the settee, leaning back against its arm, gazing up at the ceiling, wondering how the hell she always managed to mess up her life. It was men, she decided, without men life would be a doddle, a breeze. For a few months she had put her trust in a man and life had been good, but now she was back where she always seemed to be, walking that long, long corridor on her own, passing doors which this time she would certainly not even glance at let alone try and open.

She was so deep in her thoughts that she didn't hear Brett come up the stairs, didn't even realise he was there until he stood beside her. Tasha's eyes widened, but her voice was harsh as she said, 'What do *you* want?'

'To talk.' Squatting down, he took hold of her hand. 'I didn't walk out on you, if that's what you're thinking. I just needed some time and space to think. What you told me came as quite a shock.'

Taking her hand from his, Tasha swung her legs to the ground and folded her arms tightly across her chest. 'So?'

'So I want to know what *you* think about this. Whether you've decided what you want to do.'

'What do you think I ought to do?' she asked suspiciously.

'Well, I don't want to influence you in any way, but I—'

'Rubbish!' Pushing him aside, Tasha got to her feet and turned angrily to face him as he too rose. 'You've come back to persuade me to have an abortion.'

'I didn't say that. What I—'

'You didn't have to say it. The way you ran out of here—it was pathetic! You're just another man who grabs everything he can get from a woman and then takes off at the first hint of trouble. Oh, everything was fine when you finally persuaded me to have sex with you. You couldn't get enough of me then, could you? How many times a day was it? Or did you lose count? You certainly—'

Taking a swift step towards her, Brett said, 'Tasha, please stop this. I know you have a right to feel bitter but I—'

'Yes, I do damn well have the right,' she said angrily, thinking of her precious notes.

'Look, I'm sorry. I know I should have stayed, but I'm here now. Can't we talk? And before you say anything else, I want you to know that we'll do whatever you want in this. If you want to keep the baby, then that's fine by me.'

Tasha's eyes widened. 'Do you mean it?'

'Yes.' His voice was firm, but then a rueful look came into Brett's eyes. 'Though I have absolutely no idea what kind of a father I'll make.'

Tasha looked at him uncertainly, momentarily taken aback, but then an unwelcome suspicion came into her mind as she remembered that he still needed to use her material. So, playing for time, waiting for him to give himself away, she said, 'You would want to play a role in its life, then?'

'Of course.' Brett raised his eyebrows. 'You weren't expecting me to do anything else, were you?'

'I don't know. I don't know what to expect from you.' Looking at him, seeing the earnestness in his face, she couldn't believe he was the same man who had run away from the problem just hours earlier. Full of cynicism, she said, 'How—big a part do you want to play?' There was irony in her voice because Tasha didn't believe him. She was now convinced he really was playing a part, pretending to go along with her until he got what he wanted, when he would turn round and walk out again.

He gave a small shrug. 'The same as all fathers do, I suppose.' Crossing to her, he put his hands on her shoulders and looked down into her face. Smiling, he said, 'I see I have to spell it out to you. Which is understandable, I know.' His voice firm and earnest, he said, 'Yes, I do think that what's happened is wonderful, and I very much want to share it with you. I also happen to think that you are a very incredible woman, and there is no one I could possibly have chosen that I would rather have for the mother of my child.' His hands tightened a little and a look of deep tenderness came into his eyes. 'I've said that we will do whatever you want, but I very much hope that we'll set up home together as we planned.' He paused, then added deliberately, 'I want you to be happy, I want that more than anything in the world, and I very much hope that you'll marry me.'

Tasha's amazing eyes widened incredulously. 'Marry you?'

A rueful look came into his face at her astonishment. 'That is what I said.'

For a long moment she continued to stare at him, but then pushed him agitatedly away. 'That—that isn't necessary.'

'No one said it was. But it's what I want. I want it very much. And not just because of the baby, Tasha, but because I love you. I think I always have, from the moment I saw you dancing at Guy's party. You fascinated me then, and you grow more fascinating every minute.'

Whatever she had expected it certainly wasn't this. Her mouth had dropped open and Brett laughed a little as he bent to gently touch her lips with his.

'Is it so amazing?'

'Yes,' Tasha answered baldly. She had never expected him to go to these lengths. For a moment she was filled with doubt; could she possibly be wrong about him? Did he really mean it? But then she remembered his lies and the article and she grew hopelessly confused again. 'Marriage isn't an option,' she said shortly.

'Isn't it? Why not?'

'It's old-fashioned. Dated. No one needs to get married nowadays.'

'Not even if they're in love? Not even if they want to spend the rest of their lives together? Not even if they have a family?'

'No! That way you don't have the bother of a divorce when you split up.'

There was amusement in his eyes and he wasn't taking her seriously. 'What makes you think we might split up?'

'Everybody splits up, sooner or later.'

'No, they don't.' He tried to put his arms round her but she moved away. 'We'll be the exception. We have everything going for us, Tasha. We're good together.'

'The sex is good, you mean,' she said mockingly.

'Yes, it is,' Brett said evenly. 'But just being together is wonderful too. You know I want to be with you; I asked you to move in with me before. We make a good team.'

'Oh, really?'

Hearing the bitterness in her voice, Brett said, 'What is it, Tasha? Are you angry with me for making you pregnant?'

Her eyes went to his face. 'Perhaps.'

'It takes two, you know,' he pointed out evenly.

'You're blaming me.'

'It isn't a question of blame.' Brett said it as though he meant it, although inwardly he felt the innocent party in all this. 'It's happened. Maybe it was meant to be. I'm certainly very pleased about it now. I thought that you were too. I hope you are.' She looked away, wouldn't meet his eyes, so he added, 'I meant what I said, darling. I do love you. And I know that we'll be happy together.'

'You made me tell you I loved you; I didn't say it of my own free will.'

'I know that. But I think you do.'

'Why?' There was a jeering note in her voice.

Brett frowned, not understanding, but said, 'You said I was special.'

Ignoring that, Tasha said, 'And I didn't say I'd move in with you.'

Frowning again a little, he said, 'I thought that had been all agreed before we left Cornwall.'

'No. You said it was what you wanted; I didn't say I definitely would.'

He didn't agree with her, just said, 'Well, OK, but it would be the practical thing to do, wouldn't it?'

'And I certainly haven't said that I'll marry you.'

With a smile, Brett said, 'But you haven't said that you won't.'

She looked at him, thinking that this was all wrong, he hadn't been supposed to react like this. Abruptly, she said, 'I'd like you to go.'

'Without an answer?'

'You said that I gave you a shock and you had to go away and think about it. Well, you've given me an equal shock and now it's my turn to want to think.'

He nodded. 'Fair enough. But there is one thing I'd like to be sure of, Tasha; you do intend to keep this baby, don't you?'

Her mouth thinned. 'Why, is your proposal dependent on my having it?'

'No. I want to marry you whatever you decide.' He gave a grin, almost as if he was surprised at himself. 'But the idea of fatherhood is growing on me by the minute.'

Tasha flushed and lowered her eyes, not knowing what to believe, but then she raised her head and said with irony, 'I promise you, you'll be the first to know.'

'OK.' Coming to her, he kissed her again. 'You know something; I've an idea I'm extremely happy,' he said, and added, 'Don't worry, sweetheart. Everything's going to be fine.'

'Is it?'

'Yes. I'm going to look after you—both of you. Take care of you for the rest of your life.'

When he'd gone Tasha stood in the middle of the room, gazing blankly at the door through which he'd left, her thoughts in turmoil. That last thing he'd said, about him being extremely happy, she just couldn't believe. Brett was a free agent who was experienced with women, the kind of man who liked his lifestyle, his freedom to have affairs, to pick and choose. Tasha couldn't imagine him ever wanting to give that up. And besides, men like that didn't make either good husbands or fathers; they were always yearning for their lost liberty, always looking at other women until they finally stopped just looking and became unfaithful. And from what Tasha had heard they went on being unfaithful until their wives either divorced them or they became too old to be attractive to women any more. Usually the former. Tasha had been on the receiving end of enough propositions from married men to know. Not that she'd ever accepted any; it was a tacit rule among her friends that they never went with married men, never did the dirty on another woman.

She got ready for bed, but sat up against the pillows, still slightly stunned by Brett's proposal. He had seemed so sincere, as if he really meant it, but she couldn't get out of her head the possibility that he might be just kidding her along, keeping her sweet until he'd talked her into letting him use her work for his own gain. But to go to such extraordinary lengths just for that? It seemed incredible. It occurred to her that she was thinking as if she really was pregnant, but as she wasn't there was no way that she would even contemplate marrying him.

She wondered if she would have been happy if this hadn't been just a trick she'd thought up to get her revenge on Brett and she really was pregnant. It wasn't something she'd ever really thought much about. But she wouldn't have minded. It would have given a whole new meaning and purpose to life. A soft smile curved her mouth. No, she wouldn't have minded at all.

The phone rang and she picked up the receiver, expecting it to be Sarah. But it was Brett. He said, 'Hi, I thought I'd ring to make sure you're OK. Are you?'

'Of course. It's only an hour since you left,' she pointed out with some irony.

'But I've never left you in quite these circumstances before. Are you still thinking?'

For a moment she felt a pang of guilt, though why she should in the circumstances Tasha didn't know. Taking defence in coolness, she said, 'Not really.'

'Ah.' Not pushing it, Brett said, 'I didn't get round to telling you about my surprise. But I think I'll save it until the next time I see you. When will that be, do you think?'

'I don't know. I'm busy.'

There was a pause before Brett said on a puzzled note, 'I don't know what you want from me, Tasha.'

'Maybe I don't want anything.'

'That wasn't how you seemed early this evening. You seemed pretty pleased to see me again—up until the time you told me you were pregnant. Then everything seemed suddenly to change.'

'No, it changed when you walked out.' Even as she said it Tasha was appalled at herself; she was behaving as if she really was pregnant again.

'I explained about that. And I apologised. I can't do more, Tasha.'

She heard the note of warning in his voice and knew that his pride was in question here. So she said curtly, 'I don't want to talk any more. I'm tired.'

'Of course. Sleep well, then, my darling. And remember that I love you.'

Slowly she replaced the receiver, suddenly wishing with all her heart that this was for real, that neither of them was playing a deep game of their own. It could have been so good, so wonderful. But it was all a sham that left a bitter taste in the mouth, her own pretence now seeming small and petty, as humiliating as Brett's betrayal.

Switching out the light, Tasha lay back on the pillows. Only then did she realise that, having been so sure that Brett would walk out on her, it had never occurred to her that she would have to tell him that it was all a lie, that she wasn't pregnant at all.

She slept late the next day but was woken by a ring on the doorbell down in the basement area. Craning out of the front window to see who it was, she saw the local florist's van outside and yelled down at the

driver to leave what he'd brought on the doorstep.
When she finally went down, dressed for a day of first
the office and then tramping round London on an
afternoon of research, Tasha found a box on the doorstep. It contained two red roses: one in full bloom the
other still a bud. With it was a note from Brett. 'One
for each of you.'

Tasha stared at the note, somehow more overcome
with amazement and consternation now than by all
Brett's declarations of love last night. Squatting down
on the doorstep, she gazed at the flowers, then slowly
lifted out the bud and touched the soft, furled petals
with her fingertip. How could a man who'd cheated
her think to do something as kind, as *feeling,* as this?
It just didn't add up.

Sarah caught her at the office later that morning.
'Why didn't you phone and let me know what happened? You didn't chicken out, did you?'

'No. No, I told him,' Tasha answered, but felt
strangely reluctant to discuss it.

'So what happened? Surely you didn't let him talk
you round. Tasha, for heaven's sake! You didn't let
him stay the night?'

'No, of course I didn't,' she said crossly. 'What do
you take me for? Look, I can't talk now. My boss is
here,' she prevaricated. 'I'll ring you tonight. Bye.'

Leaning her elbow on her desk, Tasha looked at the
two roses that she'd brought to work with her and put
into a vase that she'd pinched from the reception area.
She was trying to work but her eyes kept going to
them, her mind to Brett. Suddenly she came to a decision. Whatever Brett had done to her, she couldn't
go on with this pretence. It belittled her, took her

down to his level. Picking up the phone, she called his house.

The answering machine came on but as soon as she said her name Brett switched the machine over and said, 'Hello, Tasha. I've been hoping you'd call.'

'I want to see you,' she said shortly. 'Can you come round to my place tonight?'

'Yes, of course. Shall I bring a take-away for us?'

'No. What I want to say won't take long. See you tonight, then.' And she replaced the receiver with a sigh of relief. Explaining, and his reaction, definitely wasn't going to be pleasant, but at least it would be off her conscience. And it would, of course, serve the purpose of finally getting rid of him for ever.

When Brett arrived she was waiting for him in the sitting-room, her arms crossed and a look of determination in her face. Seeing it, Brett at once assumed that she'd decided to have an abortion. A cold feeling stole across his heart, as if all the warmth had suddenly gone from him. Before she could speak he held up his hand and said, 'Look, I know I said that I'd abide by whatever you decided to do, but I really would like you to think really hard about this, Tasha. It isn't the end of the world. I know we're both as green as hell, but so are all parents the first time round. We'll cope, I'm sure of it,' he finished persuasively.

Tasha gave him an odd look. 'Parenthood isn't easy,' she said abruptly.

'No, I don't suppose it is. But we're mature people. I'm sure we'll work it out together.' He smiled. 'Maybe we can work together in other ways, too.'

Her eyes settled on his face. 'What had you in mind?'

'Well, with all those ideas you have, and my experience as a writer, maybe we'd make a winning combination.'

She gave a small, slightly crooked smile. 'My ideas—and your writing expertise?'

'Yes. In fact I—'

Her voice as cold and sharp as a knife blade, Tasha cut through his words to say, 'You mean your expertise gained in all the years you worked as a journalist?'

Brett's head came up sharply. Seeing the rage in her eyes, he said slowly, 'How did you find out?'

'Oh, it was quite simple.' Crossing to the shelf unit, she opened a box on one of the shelves and took the newspaper clipping from it, then held it out to him. 'I just had to read this.'

Brett glanced at it but didn't take it from her. Watching her warily, he said, 'That doesn't have my name on it.'

'But you wrote it.' She said it as a flat, definite statement, with no trace of a question in her voice.

He nodded, gave a slightly crooked grin. 'Yes—but I'd like to know how you found out.'

Having no intention of revealing her friend's part in this, Tasha said acidly, 'You made a mistake. You copied my notes verbatim, and there were a couple of sentences *I'd* written at the time, not things that Anne had told me. You really ought to check, you know, before you plagiarise other people's work.'

'You've got it all wrong. As a matter of fact this was the surprise I had for you. You see—'

But her incredulous laugh cut him off. 'You steal my work and have the sheer audacity to have it printed in a national newspaper, and then you tell me I've got it wrong! What the hell kind of moron do you take me for? Or did you think that you'd undermined my confidence enough for you to talk your way out of it?' Her face grew grim. 'Or was it just that you were convinced that I was so besotted by you that I wouldn't care?'

'If you'll just let me explain—' He tried to take hold of her hand but she shook him off.

'And just what did you mean by working together?' He hesitated and she laughed again. 'Oh, don't put yourself to the trouble of trying to think up a lie; I know darn well what your idea of our working together means; you just want to use the rest of my notes to write more articles like this. Well? Do you deny it?'

Brett looked at her for a long moment then dropped his hand. 'No, I don't deny it. That was my intention.'

Despite her knowing all along that she was right, Tasha gave an amazed gasp. 'You admit it, then?'

'Yes, because you couldn't go ahead with the exploitation programme yourself, and you wanted—'

'No, because you'd talked me out of it! God, what a fool I was to listen to you.' Tasha flung away from him, her face furious, her body rigid with anger. 'What a stupid, besotted fool!'

'Tasha, please listen to me.' Brett took a purposeful step towards her.

'Listen to you—while you talk your way out of it? Oh, no, not this time. Not now I know you for what you are.'

He came to a halt as he stared at her. His voice low, almost menacing, Brett said, 'And just what do you think I am?'

'A liar. A cheat. A plagiarist. Do you want me to go on?'

'No.' His face grew very grim. 'I think I get the message. But you couldn't be more wrong, Tasha, and if you'd just listen to me I'd prove it to you.'

Her eyes cold and contemptuous, she said, 'I'm not interested in your lies.'

Brett drew in his breath with a rasp, then said through gritted teeth, 'You don't have any choice but to be interested in me. There's the little matter of your pregnancy still between us.'

'Oh, that!' She threw him a scornful glance. 'You didn't really think I'd have the child of a swine like you, did you? No, I made that up. I wanted you to see what it was like to be on the receiving end of a lie for once.'

Brett stared at her, unable to believe his ears. For a moment he didn't believe her, thinking that she was so angry she was saying it just to punish him. But then he saw the vindictive triumph in her eyes and the dreams of the last twenty-four hours went crashing round his feet. He realised that she had planned this, had been acting a part all last night. A feeling of utter rage ran through him, an emotion more intense than any he had ever known. Catching hold of Tasha's arm, he swung her round to face him. 'I suppose you think you've been very clever. Duping me, using your cheap little trick to entrap me. And I walked right into it, didn't I? I really fell for your lies. Well, you got what you wanted. Spilling my heart out. Telling you how I felt about you.'

'Rubbish! The only reason you wanted to stay around was to persuade me to let you use the rest of my notes. My ideas, your writing expertise; that's exactly what you said.'

'And you thought I meant—' Brett broke off, then laughed bitterly. 'Boy, have you got a twisted mind.'

'Don't you dare denigrate me.' She glared at him, then said forcefully, 'This isn't about lying or cheating. This is about power. Your power over me. You thought you'd undermined my self-confidence, that you had me under your thumb and that I'd believe anything you told me, would do anything you wanted. Well, I won't! I'm free. I'm my own person. You thought that telling me you loved me would keep me sweet, would have me simpering and drooling over you. Huh! Fat chance.'

Brett's jaw grew rigid and his hands clenched into balled fists. 'Is that right? It didn't mean anything to you?'

'Oh, it meant something all right—it gave me a good laugh.'

'Really?'

She was so angry that Tasha missed the silken menace in his voice. 'Yes. You think that sex can conquer any woman, but it damn well can't!'

'That's your considered opinion, is it?' He moved closer and, too late, she saw her danger. Before she could do more than open her mouth to cry out a protest, Brett said, 'Well, let's see if you're right, shall we?' And with a quick, neat movement he picked her up and slung her over his shoulder as he carried her into the bedroom and dropped her onto the bed.

Tasha tried to fight him, but his mouth was on hers while he was pulling at her clothes. She made furious noises deep in her throat and tried to bite him, but his strength was overpowering, she had never known that a man could be that tough, that determined. She bucked and struggled but his weight held her down. She swore at him and went to scratch his face, but when she looked into his eyes Tasha became suddenly still. She had expected to see rage and fury, but his face was very cold, detached even. It took her aback and she stopped struggling, but then thought, if he can be cold then so can I, and she held herself rigid in his hold.

Deeply humiliated, Brett determined to teach her a lesson. Always before his lovemaking had been deeply passionate, with a need to arouse her as much as he himself was aroused, in a mutual search for excitement and the fulfilment of desire. But now it was different. He didn't use words to tell her how beautiful she was as he had always done before, and his kiss wasn't a means of getting close, wasn't a way of showing his need for her. Instead he used his lips merely to arouse her sensuality, as part of his insidious determination to unlock desire. Having made love to her so many times before, he knew in intimate detail just what pleased her, what excited her the most. Using that knowledge, and his own experience with women, he touched, toyed, caressed, knowing that she was determined not to give in to the deliciousness of what he was doing to her, but equally determined that she should.

They were both strong-willed people, and both were full of anger and bitterness. Tasha kept her eyes open, defying him, daring him to do his worst. His breath was hot on her skin as his lips left her mouth and moved to her neck. He found a particular spot at the base of her ear. It was a sensitive area, a place that always made her squirm with exquisite pleasure when he kissed her there, but now she resisted it. His mouth moved to her earlobe and bit gently. Ordinarily she liked that, loved it, but now she kept her head completely still, her eyes the blue of glacial ice. Brett looked at her for a moment, smiled cynically, and let his hands and his mouth move on down.

Then he was touching her skin, letting his fingers trail over her, caressing her, and she was fighting the tremors that threatened to run through her. His lips were hot, so hot, reaching into her soul for the submission he craved. Even then she tried to withstand her growing awareness, her own sensuality, but suddenly her body betrayed her. The fire of awakened sexual desire took hold, engulfed her. With a moan she stopped fighting and said, 'Yes. Oh, Brett, yes.' She moved voluptuously under his hands, wanting more, never wanting him to stop. It was exquisite, bewitching. Closing her eyes, Tasha let herself drown in the overwhelming pleasure of it, smiling as she gasped and cried out.

But to take wasn't enough, she wanted to share, and pushed aside his hand to open his shirt so that she could caress him in return. Then her hands were at his belt, pulling at his clothes, setting him free of them. She cried out with pleasure when she touched him, stroked him, then put her arms round him to hold him closer and arched her body to take him in. She was kissing his neck, had pulled off his shirt to kiss his shoulder, to bite until he cried out. It seemed a century since they had last made love. She couldn't get enough of him, couldn't get close enough, and she moaned out his name over and over again.

When she had begun to respond, when she had closed her eyes, Brett had been filled with triumph, knowing that he had won. It had been his intention, when they both knew that she couldn't resist him, to just get up and walk away, to leave her with the knowledge of her own humiliation. To make her punishment complete it had to be all one-sided, he must show no emotion at all, stay ruthlessly aloof from what he was doing to her. No less than her complete submission, her utter surrender to his caresses would do. When she reached out to touch him he tried to stop her, took hold of her hand and held it still. But the backs of her fingers brushed against his nipple, and before he knew it she had escaped him, was opening his shirt. So what the hell? he thought. If I show her that she can't reach me it will be an even bigger victory. There was still time to walk away.

Her little fingers were featherlight but wrought such havoc with his intentions. He had to stifle a groan, and against his will felt his body harden. Brett bent to caress her again, still intent on her subjugation. In just another minute he would make her look at him, make her realise that she was now the one who must beg for fulfilment, be the suppliant. And then he would show her that he no longer cared, could just turn his back on her when she needed him most. Prove to her that her sexual power over him had died with the trick she'd played on him.

But then her hands were on him and he knew that it was already too late, much too late. There was no way now that he could stop himself from loving her. It was heaven on earth. The rightness of it engulfed him along with the exquisite pleasure. And as sensuality took hold so anger and bitterness left. This was Tasha, for God's sake. The woman he had waited so long to find, who was a constant delight to his heart. They would sort it out. Nothing mattered so long as she was his, so long as they could be together like this. And he surrendered himself to her as surely as she had to him.

So what Brett had begun in anger became instead the most fantastic experience. He forgot his rage, forgot the insults she'd thrown at him, all he wanted was to please her, to carry her along with him on this wonderful road of love that he could travel only with her...only with her. It was a mountain road that climbed ever higher, reaching peak after peak until that last climb to the most glorious summit, when the world exploded into brilliant light and happiness, a beautiful dawn that seemed to last for ever.

He heard Tasha's own moans of delight and knew that he had carried her along the road with him, that her pleasure was as great as his, and he slumped down beside her, smiling with happy satisfaction.

After a while, when he could breathe properly again, Brett turned to look at her. She had her Mona Lisa smile on her mouth, that secret look of intense fulfilment, and he knew he had to try and put things right between them. 'Tasha?' Slowly she opened her eyes and looked at him. Her anger was gone and she smiled at him. 'We can't let it end like this. You must let me—'

The sound of the phone ringing cut through his words. Tasha made no move to answer it but the answering machine in the next room cut in and they heard the message clearly through the open door. 'Tasha, it's Sarah. Have you told him yet? I wish I'd been there to see his face when you told him it was all a con, that we hatched it up together. As you said, the rat certainly needed teaching a lesson. I bet he'll think twice before he tries to dupe another woman. Call me as soon as you can. I'm dying to know what happened.'

When the machine clicked off Brett swung off the bed and started pulling on his clothes. 'So you hatched this together, did you? I suppose you had a good giggle while you worked out how to make a fool of me?'

Sitting up and pulling the edges of her blouse together, Tasha said, 'I thought you'd just walk out and I'd never see you again. I never dreamed you'd—'

'Well, thanks,' Brett cut in. 'But don't mix up my standard of behaviour with your own.'

Her voice growing cold, she said, 'You can keep the notes; you didn't have to force yourself on me to get them.'

'Force?' He gave a harsh laugh as he found his shoes and pushed his feet into them. 'No one forced you, you always were a sex-cat.'

Ignoring that, she threw the biggest insult she could find at him. 'Do what you like with them. I hope they make you a lot of money. That's what you want, isn't it?'

He rounded on her and the fury in his face made her shrink back. He took his wallet from his pocket and for an appalled moment she thought he was going to throw money at her, but he pulled out a piece of paper and dropped it on the bed beside her.

'Here. This is the telephone number of the stewardess you interviewed. Yes, I got money for the article. I used it to go over there and get her, bring her back to England before the story came out. I set her up in a safe house and helped her find a new job under a new name. I thought it was your dearest wish to set her free and see her boss shown up for what he was. It was too dangerous for you to do it so I did it for you. That was the surprise I had for you.' He laughed again as he saw the growing amazement in her face. 'Not that I expect you to believe me, of course. But, you're right, one should always cross-check one's research, so why don't you phone her and let her tell you for herself? That's unless you think we've hatched up a dirty little plot together to deceive you, of course.' Then he turned and strode towards the door.

'Brett!'

But he had gone, slamming the door violently behind him.

It was a couple of months later before Brett saw Tasha again. He had gone down to Cornwall to try and work on his new book, to put the whole sordid episode out of his mind. Chalk it up to experience and make sure he never made the same mistake again. But the cottage, the beach, even the garden were too full of memories. Everywhere he turned Tasha was there, laughing at him, teasing him, in his arms as they made love. Somehow he would try to put her out of his mind, but he only had to walk into a room and smell the lingering scent of her perfume, or notice a pretty plate that she had insisted on buying for him, and he was lost again. So he had come back to London and tried to work there instead, putting the wonderful photo of her among the foxgloves firmly away in a drawer.

Until he glanced out of the window of his study one afternoon and there she was, leaning against the wall that bordered the river. He grew very still, completely dumbfounded, and as he stared she turned and looked up at his window. She didn't wave or anything, just stood and waited. For a couple of minutes he sat transfixed, all his senses reeling, his mind only slowly beginning to function. He supposed he could have ignored her, but he had spent too many hours gazing despondently at a blank computer screen over the last weeks, so he shrugged on a jacket and went out to her.

He had forgotten how lovely she was. No, not forgotten, because he had dreamed of nothing else, waking or sleeping, since they had split up, but even imagination couldn't come close to her living, breathing vitality.

'Hello, Brett.' She was studying his face but he deliberately made it mask-like, giving nothing away.

'What do you want?'

'Could we take a walk?'

He hesitated, then shrugged. 'All right.'

They began to walk along the empty riverside together but at first she didn't speak. He found that his heart was thudding in his chest and his throat was dry with tension. And he had to shove his hands in his pockets to stop them from shaking.

At last she said, 'I suppose you think I owe you an apology. Well, maybe I do, but that isn't why I came here.'

He waited for her to go on but she didn't. 'You didn't phone Anne to check on what I'd done,' he felt compelled to say, having rung the ex-stewardess himself.

'No. It wasn't—necessary.'

'Why not?'

'I believed you,' Tasha said simply. 'And I read in the paper that her boss had lost his job and been kicked off the boards of all the charities. I was really pleased about that. But you haven't written any more articles?'

'No,' he answered curtly. He made no further explanation and it really wasn't necessary; she knew he wouldn't touch her research after what had happened between them.

'I've been thinking in these last weeks,' she remarked. 'On life, that kind of thing.'

'Is that what you've come to talk about?'

'Yes, partly.'

'And your conclusions?' Brett deliberately let his voice sound bored.

'I've realised that the warmth and love of another human being is what we all live for.'

'Very original,' he said with heavy sarcasm.

She glanced at him, gave a small smile. 'And I also

learned that sex is important, vitally important in a relationship. It can be the difference between leading a happy, fulfilled life or an unfulfilled life.'

'It always has been.'

'But I mean good sex. The kind of sex we had together,' she added deliberately.

Brett was silent for a moment, his face taut, then he said roughly, 'What are you leading up to, Tasha?'

'You once said that you loved me, asked me to marry you.'

'The circumstances have changed,' he said shortly.

'Well, no, actually, they haven't.'

He frowned. 'What do you mean?'

'I'm pregnant.'

Coming to a jolting stop, he swung round on her, instantaneous anger in his eyes. 'If you think you can pull that trick twice then you can...' His voice trailed off as he looked into her face and saw the radiance in her eyes. Slowly he let out his breath. 'My God, you mean it.'

'Yes.'

His eyes grew cold. 'Congratulations. Who's the proud father?'

She laughed. 'I suppose I deserved that.' But she wasn't at all put out. 'It was a rotten trick to pull, wasn't it? But I thought you'd done the dirty on me, you see. That you were just another rat of a journalist who would do anything for a story. I'm afraid I forgot for a while that you were—well, you.' She looked at him but his chin was still up, his mouth set into a thin, resolute line. Ignoring it, Tasha went on, 'It was that last time that did it, when you were so determined to teach me a lesson and instead it turned out to be such fabulous love.'

'Until the phone rang,' he pointed out acidly.

'Oh, yes. Sarah. She's found a new boyfriend, by the way.'

'Good, maybe she'll keep her nose out of other people's business for a change.'

Tasha smiled, and said casually, 'The answer's yes, by the way.'

'What?' He was still thinking venomously about that she-devil Sarah, sure that Tasha would never have had the idea at all if it hadn't been for her.

'Yes, I will marry you. And as soon as possible, please.'

He gasped incredulously. 'Do you think—?'

'That you still want to marry me? Yes, of course you do.'

Brett stared in disbelief, then saw perfect certainty in her eyes and slowly began to laugh. 'Yes,' he agreed. 'Of course I do.' And he swept her into his arms and kissed her, kissed her so deeply that they were both out of breath when he finally let her go. Then he grinned. 'Well, at least I wasn't completely floored this time.' Putting his arms possessively round her, he said, 'Do you know what made me realise how much I loved you and how much I wanted you to have the baby last time?' When she shook her head, he went on, 'I was thinking of all the terrible things I'd heard about fatherhood, but I suddenly saw in my mind a little girl with your hair and your incredible eyes, smiling at me and holding her arms out to me. And then I was completely hooked.'

'Good, I'm glad.' She reached up to kiss him. 'I've missed you.'

'Would you have come back to me if this hadn't happened?' he asked tensely, afraid of what she might say.

'Yes, of course, you idiot. But I had a lot of thinking to do first, a lot of self-accusations to answer. I made the terrible mistake of lumping all journalists together instead of following my instincts, my own heart when it told me that I was in love with you.'

'Well, that's nice to know. You've never said that before.'

'Of course I have. You were too busy reaching a climax to listen.' He let that go and she said, 'Now will you write the rest of that series?'

Brett raised an eyebrow. 'Do I have the copyright owner's permission?'

'Definitely. But only if you promise to do the story on my old college tutor first.'

That made him burst into laughter. Lifting her off her feet, he said with intense happiness, 'I can see I'm going to get into constant trouble with you around.'

Tasha smiled down at him. 'But at least you'll never be bored.'

'No. Never that.'

He kissed her again, and Tasha found herself at the end of the corridor and stepping into a golden morning that would stretch for ever. With a sigh of content she firmly closed the door behind her and walked confidently into the future.

MILLS & BOON®

Next Month's Romances

♡

Each month you can choose from a wide variety of romance novels from Mills & Boon. Below are the new titles to look out for next month from the Presents and Enchanted series.

Presents™

AN IDEAL MARRIAGE?	Helen Bianchin
SECOND MARRIAGE	Helen Brooks
TIGER, TIGER	Robyn Donald
SEDUCING NELL	Sandra Field
MISTRESS AND MOTHER	Lynne Graham
HUSBAND NOT INCLUDED!	Mary Lyons
THE LOVE-CHILD	Kathryn Ross
THE RANCHER'S MISTRESS	Kay Thorpe

Enchanted™

TAMING A HUSBAND	Elizabeth Duke
BARGAINING WITH THE BOSS	Catherine George
BRANNIGAN'S BABY	Grace Green
WAITING FOR MR WONDERFUL	Stephanie Howard
THE WAY TO A MAN'S HEART	Debbie Macomber
NO ACCOUNTING FOR LOVE	Eva Rutland
GEORGIA AND THE TYCOON	Margaret Way
KIT AND THE COWBOY	Rebecca Winters

JASMINE CRESSWELL

Internationally-acclaimed Bestselling Author

SECRET SINS

The rich are different—they're deadly!

Judge Victor Rodier is a powerful and
dangerous man. At the age of twenty-seven,
Jessica Marie Pazmany is confronted with
terrifying evidence that her real name is
Liliana Rodier. A threat on her life prompts
Jessica to seek an appointment with her
father—a meeting she may live to regret.

**AVAILABLE IN PAPERBACK
FROM JULY 1997**